CONDITIONS UNCERTAIN
AND LIKELY TO PASS AWAY

tales by
Frank Stanford

CONDITIONS UNCERTAIN AND LIKELY TO PASS AWAY

Lost Roads   Number 37   Providence   1990

Library of Congress Cataloging in Publication Data
Stanford, Frank, 1948–1978   Conditions uncertain and likely to pass away:
tales by Frank Stanford
   (Lost Roads series; no. 37)
   I. Title
PS3569.T3316C65   1990   813'.54—dc20
ISBN 0-918786-42-8

This is a work of fiction. Names, characters, places and incidents are either the product of the author's imagination or are used fictitiously. Any resemblance to actual persons, living or dead, events, or locales is entirely coincidental.

Copyright © 1971–1978 Frank Stanford
Copyright © 1978–1981 Estate of Frank Stanford
Copyright © 1981–1990, C.D. Wright
P.O. Box 5848 Weybosset Hill Station
Providence, Rhode Island 02903
Typeset by Typeworks, Inc., Belfast, Maine

Cover painting "Happiness A Little Forced" by John Stoss
Book design by C.D. Wright and Forrest Gander

This project is supported with funds donated by Deborah Luster and Michael Luster. The editors wish to extend a special thanks to them for their generosity in helping to bring these tales to light.

Poetry by Frank Stanford

The Singing Knives (Mill Mountain Press 1921)   OP*
Shade (Mill Mountain Press, 1973)   OP
Ladies From Hell (Mill Mountain Press, 1974)   OP
Field Talk (Mill Mountain Press, 1975)   OP
Arkansas Bench Stone (Mill Mountain Press, 1975)   OP
Constant Stranger (Mill Mountain Press, 1976)   OP
The Battlefield Where The Moon Says I Love You (Mill Mountain Press/
    Lost Roads Publishers, 1977)   OP
The Singing Knives (Lost Roads Publishers, 1979)
You (Lost Roads Publishers, 1979)   OP
Crib Death (Ironwood Press, 1979)   OP
The Selected Poems of Frank Stanford (University of Arkansas Press, 1991)

*OP: out of print

NOTES ON THE TALES

At the bottom of the final page of "Ansar's Tale and Luper's Note" the author has written with a red pen: "Back in the saddle again Tooty toot toot We have big fun on the bayou" indicating either there had been a lapse in his writing time or that he felt he was "hitting" once again, the latter more probable, as he was never to my knowledge, not writing.

"Ben Fallow's Tale" is accompanied by an alternate title on one xeroxed copy, "Legend of a Poet," and with the following typed note: "(The balance of III is 16 pages. The balance of IV is 30 pages.) I'm revising the last part, so as to make IV a little longer and self-contained, in hopes of publishing it as a story. Although I might be contradicting Goethe, neither my dramatic or epic sense wants to leave this a 100 page story. I'd like to sink some time in it."

On the title page of "Delainy's Tale" the author has penned "This Light" possibly as a new title consideration. However he has not scratched the typed title (Delainy's Tale), and on the first page of the story he has again penciled the title "Delainy's Tale."

The enclosed tales do not represent a true selection of all the extant Stanford stories, but a majority of the stories to which I hold the rights. The rights to other uncollected stories by Frank Stanford are held by the poet's widow, Ginny Crouch Stanford.

Except where intention is obviously at risk, the author's spelling and punctuation, whether deliberately or inadvertently variant, is retained. Occasional glitches, including word omissions and abortive sentences, duplicate the late Stanford's typescript and thereby reflect his hand in the rough.

CONTENTS

Conditions Uncertain And Likely To Pass Away:
McQuistion's Tale   9

DeMoss's Tale   15

The Son's Tale   19

Kimpel's Tale   23

Delainy's Tale   29

Hitchcock's Tale   36

Ansar's Tale & Luper's Note   47

The Fool's Tale   56

Merton's Tale   62

Ben Fallow's Tale   82

Surtees' Tale   120

1.

McQUISTION'S TALE

One's country is a group of rivers that flow into the sea. The sea that is death. There you are . . . to die for one's country.
  Luis Buñuel

No man knows that the stranger he meets coming out of the forest in a new country is not already an invisible member of Christ and perhaps one who has some providential or prophetic message to utter.
  Thomas Merton

McQuistion's Tale

I went down the road to have supper with Shing. My feet were so pale and warm from the dust when I got there that I pumped water on them, I pumped water over myself, letting it run down over my bare chest and under the belt of my shorts. I stood in the ditch like a wheel. Wearing no drawers, the water went freely down my legs, and the evening wind crawled up under the loose fitting hand-me-down cut-down pants. I had just come from the Greek's tugboat, and the swarthy and enchanted music he played was still with me, and not even the low wind could make me listen to another thing.

"Did you hear that?" Shing asked me.

"What was it that you heard?"

"Those womens whispering in the kitchen."

"Where are you?"

"I'm in the tree with the cat. He chased the snake up here."

"I'll help you down; I came to eat with you."

"Yes, it's good that a young man today can remember an old man of yesterday. And how are your teeth? Don't let them go bad like mine. Your mouth is pretty and white, I suppose. You better watch that one dark tooth. Everything rots."

"Did I . . . ."

"Did I get a letter?"

"Did I leave my book here? No, there wasn't anything up at the store."

"Black mail, stones in my pathway, are you hungry?"

Shing had lost his sight before he had ever known he was entitled to such a thing. He was born without eyes. A long time ago all they had was two shining orbs, like ball bearings, and so the government sent him enough money to buy them. And now it's like looking into bent mirrors. Poor Shing, he was losing his mind like a pond losing water in a dry summer. He said things you knew weren't true. Like he said he had a son named Woe. He was a ventriloquist and his dummy was named Arimathea. Who would believe that?

Shing had a bad habit of yelling at people when they came by. I was afraid they'd come and get him. They took up a special collection in the church to pay the deputy to leave him alone. The only thing he ever did that was real bad was come to the wedding naked with his white Persian cat. A man drove his tractor to town and said he saw a naked nigger walking down the road with a rod and a cat. They got the man down off the John Deere and took him into the beer joint. No matter, Shing was alright. Everybody else was going broke from bad crops, and going crazy from that. It was the blood in Shing's veins. It was getting hard as okra when it doesn't rain.

"I know, I know," he said, climbing down the tree, "you're fixing to tell old Shing so long; I know, you got a new buddy, that Greek on the river, and I don't blame you; I see what you're getting at, you're looking at that sawdust falling out of my leg, I'm worse off than Joseph of Arimathea, that dummy, so say so long."

"I mighty hungry, Shing."

His big cat was coughing up the feathers hanging from its mouth. A cricket was sitting on the edge of a pail in the corner of his porch, and it wouldn't jump for anything. The wind made the swing creak, so I got a can of Three-In-One oil and wet the chain and the eyes screwed into the ceiling. He shaved by the window. There was a sock draping his mirror. After so many years the suds from the cakes of soap had filled up the sill like snow. It looked like a slab of salt pork. There were some chinese chimes hanging down from the roof of his porch and when there was no wind he used a fan to blow them together. There were some dominoes in a wooden box on his table but I never played with him because he cheated. Just because he was blind you figured he wouldn't cheat you, but he had them filed down some way where he couldn't lose. There were blue bottles from Milk of Magnesia and Vapor Rub all over. He liked blue. He'd pick the mud dobbers out of their nests and listen to them buzz. He said, "If I had eyes, I wished they'd be blue as dirt dobber wings when they flutter so fast." People used to set their clocks in the windows at night, but he came around and stole them.

"What will we have?"

"Go get the ladle and taste it."

"Did you see my letter? I want you to mail it tomorrow."

"God, it's hot out tonight, isn't it Shing?"

"When you bury me, I want the moon to be on my rosary. See if anybody will go in on a pyramid. I want a picture by what's his name; one of those high-yellows eating a watermelon. And there's one where she's lying on her belly with a flower in her hair and a black ghost is hiding behind her. Carry my mahogany outside by the tree, don't let the outhouse smell too much, say No, take your waking slow."

I walked into the kitchen.

"It's a beetree in there somewhere. Where that wine at?"

It was hot. I stood up on a bottle case, dipped some of the stew up, and, as I blew on the spoon my sweat dripped into the black cauldron. The bottle case quivered. I went back outside and sat down on the swing with him. He cooled himself with a fan that came from church. A big eye was drawn on it, right in the center of a pyramid. He was sweating terrible. *Be not forgetful to entertain strangers, for thereby some have seen to angels unawares* was written on the other side of the fan with *HEBREWS 13:1–2*.

"It's nice when the sun goes down," I said.

"You bet your boots. It's nice at night. You shut the door, the footsteps die."

"Did you ever find your friend?" I asked him.

"No. He must have gotten drunk, and walked off to the woods and died. Ha-ha."

"He might have stepped off in the quickmud. You know what happened to the catskinner?"

"They never found the bulldozer, either. They let down anchors in the earth and never touched anything. The mud is so deep. Deeper than my mother's lamp that I carried for the ghosts in the hollow. You can't fool Shing. And here I came like a shadow that wasn't looking where it was going. Ain't old Shing a sight?"

"I was hoping you would tell me a story before supper, Shing."

"I'm scared a lonely. Ha-ha. Get that Greek to coo. Ha-ha."

"What about one for old time's sake?"

"Shit. I was hoping you'd tell me who's been stealing the cornbread off my backporch. It's them womens."

"Maybe an animal?"

"Ha. Animal don't leave wrappers. Don't smell like rancid butter. Animal know when a gut is too little to be saved. I won't mention anymore. Except there was a moon and her hair was like wheat."

"Somebody brings their own butter, then steals your bread. That is a story."

"A dog wouldn't smell like that. No boy, that is the truth. I got to quit calling you that. Is the ladder still up side the beetree, is there a clean room for the visitors?"

We ate hot food for such a warm night. "I don't see how the Mexicans do it," I told him. He drank a bottle of Tabasco, and started hollering. I had to drink four Nehis. One of them I chipped the neck off the bottle. Shing said there was liable to be more glass around, so he had me strain it through a minnow sieve. He didn't know a small piece of glass could even get through that. Somebody went by and called on us he was yelling so loud.

"Sometimes," he said, "you can stop dead in your tracks and hear your footsteps go on."

A wagon came by, the white dust splashing through the spokes of the wheels like flour through a woman's hands. Shing put the broken neck of the bottle on his finger.

"Is there two people in that rig?"

"There are," I said.

"Is one tall and the other short?"

"Yes."

"My son Woe, and his dummy, Joseph of Arimathea."

2.

DeMOSS'S TALE

DeMoss's Tale

Silent Night told them he would take me to town in his Ice Truck and get my hair cut. He told the boss this so he could go see THE DEVIL. He'd come to town with the carnival. There was a poster on the light pole across from the store that told about him.

"Now how I'm going to keep a load of ice all day on the truck?" Silent Night asked me. "They won't have none left this afternoon and the new ice won't be ready yet."

"Why don't you pay for it this morning and pick it up when we leave this evening." He liked for me to answer questions he already knew the answers to.

"You're thinking. I'll get Rudy to cut your hair, too."

"Rudy, hell. Rudy at the Ice House?" Since when does he know how to cut hair? I want these ears to stay on my head."

"He does, he does. Never you mind."

Going into the Ice House in the summer was like sleeping in a dark hollow. There was a coolness that sunk into your eyes like those Auto Parts calendars of naked women. It was like a palace in the desert of the delta. They said there was a dead girl frozen there. They say she drowned in a pond one winter, and back in the days when they got their ice like that — naturally from the winters and the waters, they cut her out with the picks and saved her. She was supposed to be in the back, hidden somewhere in a block clear as a bell. But I never payed much attention to all those stories; I thought they were all made up by old men who drink and wander.

I sat down on a cold crossbeam, the nicks and gashes of which had been filled with water and frozen. All along the board there was evidence of rind, scales, fur, and blood, even some strawberry ice cream. As Silent Night dozed on a block of frost-bitten knuckles, I listened to Rudy cut my hair. I ate some of his soda crackers. My curls fell down in the sawdust, and when someone opened the thick door to the locker the window blew them over the ice. I thought about how many thirsty people would be drinking my hair. They'd be picking strands out of their mouths like bones in a fish.

Rudy put up his scissors and woke Silent Night. "Two-bits, friend."

"Let's throw to the line for it," Silent Night told him.

The two of them went outside in the heat and gambled, while I looked for the place they kept the ice cream and melons. Wouldn't Shing like an Eskimo Pie every evening I thought, looking under the damp canvas. I was going to steal a case of them if I could. Sometimes the Ice House reminded me of the ship of death, and I was on it, drifting somewhere around the South Pole. It reminded me of the sea stories The Swede told, burials at sea, and women like figureheads frozen to the prows. I like to rip open melons, as if they were bellies of evil.

Something shined in one of the blocks of ice, like a quarter. I got a pick and cut the corner off. I put it in my pocket. It was cold like dry ice, like the shaving mirror on Shing's window sill whenever I walked down the road in winter to catch the schoolbus.

"Come on, let's go see the devil," Silent Night said, opening the locker door. The light outside made you sick. It hurt my eyes and my belly spun around like a run-over rabbit.

When you gave the man at the carnival the money to see The Devil, you had to go in alone. They made you wait in a little anteroom, part of the entrance to the tent. They had a tape recorder going with the sound effects of wind. A woman, dressed like they do in show business, appeared and asked you whether or not there was something in your past you were ashamed of, something you wouldn't want the Devil to know. She asked you to write it down. If you couldn't write, there was a sign which said she would write it for you. I never did understand that. I sat down on the bench they had and thought. The woman smelled like perfume and sweat. Somebody said something on the other side of the tent flap, so she tapped on it with her hand and leaned her ear to it. She was very tall, almost seven feet. She didn't know that as she whispered to the other voice she was leaning her body against mine. I could see the veins and bruises on her legs. Part of her behind was showing. I touched the dimple of her muscle with my finger. I ran it across the curve of her hip, just where she was coming out of the bathing suit. She went, "Ooo!" She reached in my left pocket and turned it inside out. Nothing but crumbs. She looked down at me over the feathers around her bosom. I could smell it thawing. I think someone was looking at us through a hole in the canvas. It could of been a spider. I spit at it. She reached into my other pocket, no change at all; nothing but the cold, dead minnow. I put the pencil on the end of my tongue and wrote down the name of my cousin. He was the one who gave me the pair of pants.

3.

THE SON'S TALE

The Son's Tale

I am blind and so in some things I will not be as good as my father, while in others I will be better. I cannot read some of the books he could, but I have women read them to me. Many thought him a good-looking oaf, unable to read at all, but that was just part of his act, part of the deal he made. In fact, I'm told that in something he was supposed to be the best at, I have him. Strange, but true, he and I had the same mistress, and she told me so. Some of the people who have gone up in the world — professors, writers, and wealthy, well-educated people — have made their reputations and fashionable points and books by calling my father many things: country bumpkin, shitfarmer, gardener of passion, anti-intellectual, and so on.

One of the last letters I received from his last mistress, my first lover, said: "You were formed in a desert in America. Come to England, Europe, San Francisco, or New York if you wish, but it is my advice that you stay where you are. I have tried all my life to live in and about the fire of animals and those who live close to the earth, as the old gray beard said, but you, dear son, will never have to try, like me, to do these things, you will, like your father, have it come naturally to you." And she enclosed a letter from him: "Do not give up your leaves unless you intend to spend the seasons waiting. I learned my life from the beasts and their abode, and I was only able to teach a bird and a few horses and a dog very little.

Many things from them, nothing in return. I broke the horses for fine ladies to ride, beat the dogs so they wouldn't kill well-kept foul, and I cut the bird's wings and split its tongue and it only said one thing, 'Farewell.' Ah, lad, I know how you'll turn out, flame far from the candles. Now you're bound to know of that old fool from Vermont who said the only good mule was a mule in a harness. Do you hear that, lad? Making love and art a hard day's work for the man and the beast of burden. It is not right. Oh, a little haying, a little cleaning in the barnyard, but a good poem can't share the same traces with a mule. Do you hear that, lad? I'll tell you why. Listen up. All the old fool's fields are barren now, and his mule is still living, but a mule cannot procreate itself. I told one man what I thought and look what he did. Don't let a soul do your looking for you. There will be no celibate dreamer telling my son what to do, and I do not want you talking to writers. They're a bad lot, lazy, and unused to labor and good love. They have called me widowrobber and wifestealer and firebrand who thinks he can pull and guide his plow through the fields himself. They say I'm too smart for me breeches, but I wonder at what they are saying when they also say I can't read my own name. And God knows what all they'll say after I'm dead. I thought he was a good man that one I talked to. He kept hanging around, asking things a man only talks to a woman. He was an odd one, sad and serious all the time. He couldn't even drink. But they can throw his books in the fire, and we'll both survive. Him and me. You know I'm not supposed to be a real man, only in words. But look at you. I got a name and it got around. I did my strutting before you were born, and now I'm what's become, what's become of the mulch on your garden. Ah, lad, these men will all slip on the ice in their buildings, they'll turn to bad reading at night when they should be loving, and they'll re-hire that old interior decorator Whittier to spruce up the sun. But you keep your wits about you, boy. You hear that? I want you always to have the smell of the ground about you, with its flowers and manure, the musk of a woman on your hands, and I want your clothes to smell like whoever you are. Careful now.

I never want you to have another man or a woman's blood on those hands, as I did. Don't let me down. Mellors."

Sometimes my house is quiet as a fisherman fishing alone. When I remember the mornings, I only remember the mornings. If I was gathering eggs in the cold in my black coat. If I was teaching the children sleep. If I was dreaming what it is to be a woman. If I was dreaming of a delicate woman, bad and quiet, playing the samisen, looking at me as if I were several plums close together like a cluster within reaching distance on the branch; thinking of the lunar dust of her face, and how her fingers were like feathers, and when I heard the silence of the mill wheel not turning, and the wild turkeys not drinking, and I knew they had hypnotized themselves in the stream, drinking their morning water. The mornings I spend like the time one takes to put on a new bandage, a dime to call a bank for the weather long distance.

The women come here from the cities to write the stories. They have read the books, seen the movies. They want to beat some more dust out of the sun, that old rug.

I got out of bed, knelt, saying a few quick songs to the spirits of the fish I had eaten the night before, and took the sword from its bamboo resting place, out of the silk sheath, holding it up to the window, feeling to see if the sun was there, how high in the sky by the glare on the edge of the blade, the heat on my face. I talk like a blind man.

It was the third morning in a row I had slept late, the one who usually wakes, the child up the road, having drowned. Some birds are beautiful, but they are as dumb as the gods. Peacocks will drown themselves looking at the rain, and if there is no wind, the blue Andalusian rooster will keel over in a tiny pool from staring at itself. I've given up on the birds of prey; some of my hawks had heart attacks from wanting to kill, and they learned to love the meat in my wrist. There was one, beautiful eagle left in a cave on a rocky cliff above Hurricane River, but I jilted the taxidermist's daughter, and the story is far too long.

4.
KIMPEL'S TALE

Kimpel's Tale

Michael had Wheat load his iron bed on the truck and take it to the edge of the water. "What did he do that for," Rigoletto asked Burdock.

"You are always asking me questions about a man I don't know. Why, I don't have any idea what color his eyes are. I know nothing of him." This is what Burdock told Rigoletto as he weighed his catch.

The next day Wheat came with a phonograph and a large straw hat. The brim was wider than a woman's. Rigoletto went on scraping the mess off the hull of his boat. He had on high trousers of good cloth, suspenders, and a black T-shirt. Morning wasn't gone yet. The clouds rolled down the sky like bales of cotton on a catwalk. "Burdock, there is no wonder in your blood. If you cut open the fish and they was pocketwatch in the belly, you wouldn't want to know whose it was. Would you?"

"Look. You get a cut of the money. You're no different from Wheat. He does things, whatever Michael asks him — and then wants to know — from me — if he should have done them. He could open a whorehouse, build a church. I don't care. I wish you two would leave me be, let me work, and let Michael what's his name do what he pleases. You don't see me talking all day. I work."

There was no mud in the river, no loose sand. The channels were clear, and there were enough fish to catch and sell. Sometimes in the fall, Rigoletto liked to tell the same story again. He left some place late one night, really early on a Sunday morning before light. He had had too much to drink and was sleepy at the wheel. "I was going to sleep, but a hawk flew off a fence post, right up into the headlights. Scared the devil out of me. Burdock, I wouldn't be here today if it hadn't been for that creature." There were streaks of white oil on Rigoletto's ears from his hair tonic. He smelled like fish and lavender. He smoked the small cigarillos down to where they scorched his fingers, and he played with his thick lips with his thumb.

"You shouldn't have been driving so late. Where were you going?"

"It was Sunday morning I told you. I had to be there by five so I could go out in the boat by six. I had to take the boat that day, not the skiff."

The next few weeks Rigoletto hardly spoke at work. He liked to be alone. He did twice his share, just so he wouldn't have to be with the others. There was no one there, but he seemed to be in the midst of someone else. Far away on the island, Burdock could hear Sis Woman singing gospel songs.

"Worrywart, how come you haven't asked me anything about Michael in so long," Burdock asked Rigoletto, intruding on the other's new quiet way of working, trying to cover in another tone the sincerity of his question. "Wheat hardly speaks to me anymore. What's with ya'll?" Rigoletto tied the hook on the line without answering.

The next day at work the silence was still the same. Only Burdock's voice was heard. He felt he was making a fool of himself. When they came in that evening he said, "I have a feeling something is going to give. I had this feeling once before when I was a kid. I got up out of my bed, walked down the stairs, went into the corner of the big room, and waited. A guitar string broke. Just busted. I walked back upstairs and went to sleep. The next day, my folks found fingerprints on the guitar. They tried to blame me. Now isn't that some story?" But Rigoletto never said a word, he didn't look his way. It was he who usually rode in the bow and jumped out on the bank first to tie up. But this time Rigoletto got out in the knee-deep water and walked towards his truck and drove off, as if Burdock wasn't there. But Burdock didn't call back; he wanted to, but he didn't. He looked down at the slick bellies of the fish. He felt humiliated, as if he'd passed wind at a funeral. All he was and all he had set in on his mind like wilt on his garden. He thought about the lousy junk cluttering his house — but he loved it, the phrases he threw out the door of his mouth to the people he saw everyday. He looked over the side of the boat into the clear, still water. He saw how the black heads had taken over his nose and the sides of his temples. He'd forgotten where to wash, if his mouth smelled like sourdough. His teeth were dark, dirty as a grease monkey's fingernails. The last woman he'd slept with he hadn't tried anything with. He just kept changing the stations on the radio as they went off the air, one by one.

He stood up in the boat and unzipped his pants. He shouted so loud Sis Woman could hear him. He took off his glove and pulled out his member and pissed in the water. His hand was cold. The steam rose off his water. It was cold as hell, he thought.

He walked over to the iron bed on the beach, now, half buried in the sand. So was the phonograph, and the wide-brimmed hat was rotting. It was a beautiful, light hat. He began cleaning the fish. The blood and slime on the board was like a cold pudding. He heard a steady, almost ticking sound; a small hole in the bottom of a boat makes that sound, he thought, but it was nothing — nothing to worry over. A scale flew up in his eye. He couldn't get it out. He worked with one eye shut. As soon as Rigoletto showed up he'd ask him about Michael. He might even stop by Wheat's place that evening. He couldn't wait for tomorrow's work to roll around. The next day he'd tell them all the things he'd wanted to. He looked around in the dark fog with one eye open, and his hundred pounds of fish in a sack on his back. The next day he'd smile and speak his peace. He thought he saw something glowing in the bucket of guts.

Rigoletto didn't show up the next morning. So Burdock went out alone. It snowed in his boat and he drew more and more water. He fished all day and he spoke to Sis Woman. She was wrapped up on the beach in front of the fire in a big fur coat a preacher had given her. She was drinking wine and hollering. His other eye was still filled with something. It was as if the afternoon was a cold, swollen belly and his eye was the point of something sharp. It kept snowing and he rowed in with his catch.

He wouldn't have to clean them, he thought; they would keep in the cold. He sat in the old bed long enough to get a cough, and for no reason at all he howled like a coyote. The black crows took turns waiting for him to leave, walking around the rim of the bucket, the bucket full of eyes and guts. The snow disappeared in his black coat. He looked at the ice covering the dry rot setting in on his boat, where the wood was getting soft around the name on the bow. There was sandpaper at the house, he thought. He got up and the crows flew away. He put the skiff on his back, like a shell, and walked up the steep hill to his place. He was awkward, but he was getting his job done. He would have liked to have had help. He pulled the boat up the steps into the doorway, bow first and upturned. It wouldn't go any further, and neither could he. He put wood in the stove and water in the pot. He would have liked someone to have been there and for the house to be warm. He would burn a lot of wood that night, he thought, because he would have to work on the boat late, and the air would come in the door. He lit his pipe, not knowing where to begin: should he start with the name on the bow or should he sand the keel and the bottom? He looked around his room; there wasn't a picture of anyone, not even a snapshot of himself. The coating of ice had melted. *To hell with it,* he thought out loud. He sanded just a few inches around either side of the prow. Let the rest go, he thought. He dipped a small brush in a bottle of blue paint and went to work on the letters. But he just couldn't get it right. Then he began to change the name, not the way he painted it. It would look good on one side, only for him to paint another name on the opposite side. He worked till late.

Up the road, he could hear music and laughter coming from Michael's place. And the snow kept falling in the quiet night. He thought he saw Rigoletto's truck pulled out in front. He kept looking up at the time, said there was something he hadn't done, something he had to do. He had to sit close to the stove while he thought. If there was another name, he had to think of it. He could see the cold night coming through his door.

5.

DELAINY'S TALE

Delainy's Tale

"Midnight was when it was."
"True, true."
"Larkspur had done the painting for me: *Idea of My Father as a Young Man*. He knew him then you see."
"I see."
"It was hung from the hook I forged to get the big fish."
"You caught it and burned it."
"I burned it in the barn. Would you like some more whiskey in your jar?"
"No thanks, Delainy. The horses ran out on fire?"
"The mare's mane was burning; she was about to foal."
"She jumped over the barb-wire into the pond."
"And Lester threw a rope around her."
"We pulled her out."
"You pulled her out? Lester took the knife out of his boot and cut through the belly."
"I couldn't see the white on the colt – the Appaloosa. Too much blood."
"Blood of the mother and blood of the born."
"Lester gave the colt to me."
"To you!"
"You could see the barn glowing in the dead mother's eyes."
"The barn looked like a ship – a comet."

"There was a boat come up the river like that, long ago. I've heard."

"You mean the shipwreck in Dominic's Lagoon?"

"I mean that."

"That morning Sinda smelled like a fish."

"The tote-sack burned off it . . . like dust, like the dust on its skin. Like a wick."

"My wife — oh Jesus kiss her sweet feet — was dusting the mirror. It came then. I ain't lying."

"No, not then Delainy; it came when Sara Bundy poked out her eye with the willow switch."

"You are right. Boy, do me a favor. Go into the place and bring me a tin of sardines. Delainy, he want to eat his fish now. And get a lemon, too. Damn, and bring salt. I'll put more whiskey in your jar, I'll make you a good drink. Lemon juice, and the sardine oil, and the whiskey."

"Here you are. Now tell. It sounds better when you tell about your dream before you tell about when it came."

"These dreams man. Death has the loud pipes on its limosine, black rhinestones on the mudflaps. Look — whose guitar is that floating down the river? Roscoe's wife, she threw it in the water. But I tell you now: The boy was cutting stove wood outside. . . ."

"Little chinks flying up!"

". . . My feet looked like two crows at the end of the bed."

"You had the blanket caddie-cornered."

"I smelled the bacon and the coffee. I smelled the sorghum and the Royal Lyme Perfume."

"We found a crate of it in the shipwreck."

"Some wanted the Bay Rum in the brown bottles."

"Some took the Lyme in the green bottles."

"And in your dream you couldn't tell if the moon was going down. . . ."

". . . Or the sun was coming up."

"But there was ochre in the mirror and in the dust floating in the room."

"And the cats were eating the dead minnows in the live box under the house."

"You took out your watch."

"I took it out of my britches. I slept that night, I slept with my pants on. I felt the watch ticking against me all night like a grasshopper nailing a coffin."

"Then you. . . ."

". . . Opened it. The facing went back slow. . . ."

". . . Because of the bad spring. . . ."

". . . And caught a little of the dark, red light. I saw Sinda eating in the charred barn, eating the fish meat with a fork. You could see through the bones."

"And that's when your wife brought you your juice and told you one of the boats were loose?"

"Yes. I drank it, then I reached under the mattress for the bottle. First, I felt the 32-22, then the bottle. I drank a long drink, too. She asked me what time it was. I said, 'Water has gotten in here. I can't tell you.' She left."

"Then you heard the rowing."

"The sound of oars. I got out of my bed, put on my boots. I didn't feel a need for clothes. It wasn't that cold. My longjohns would do. And I took my watch."

"You opened the trapdoor."

"Then climbed down the ladder and knocked down a few mud dobber nests. A man in a boat. No fisherman I knew. He threw me a line. The rope was wet and soggy."

"It felt like a dead snake?"

"He'd been dragging it through the water for a long time it seemed. 'Greetings friend,' he said. 'Let me introduce myself. The name is. . . .'"

"You still can't remember the name?"

"I try. I try. He was – a – comedian – a great comedian."

"What did he look like?"

"Not funny. Not funny at all."

"And his boat had a strange name?"

"Yes, it was his all right; no one around here to rent one like that. No boat like that on these waters. Across the bow in a good hand was written: THE SETTING."

"Like the sun."

"Yes."

"What did it mean, Delainy? Did it mean the day and the night? The Setting. It could mean like a supper."

"I couldn't tell you — not if I tried."

"What else did he say?"

"I'm not sure. Both hands of my watch, they meeting at twelve. The light commence to be odd."

"Did he give a warning?"

"I don't know. His voice was like three men in the shadows — you know — like a echo. Men speaking news over a lantern held down to the water. His clothes were old and worn. And dark. Very dark."

"No bright shirt like a man on a vacation wears?"

"No."

"He was. . . ."

". . . A strange comedian."

"Just what I was about to say. Listen, could I have something to eat. I didn't have breakfast."

Delainy got me a piece of cornbread and a bruised apple. He put wood on the stove, and I ate as he warmed his hands, looking back over his shoulder at me. All around his shack I noticed levels, carpenters' levels. They were in place to tell him when the dead logs and oil drums, which kept him afloat, settled to the bottom. He said he could go anytime. Sinking was quick. None of the bubbles were even. I was quick to point this out to him, but he took it all in stride.

The wind had sucked the toilet paper out of the holes in the screens. He lit his pipe, stirring the match with his thumbnail.

"What about some music?"

My mouth was full of bread and buttermilk, so I nodded yes. He got a record out of his chest. He blew the dust off it. It was one of those brittle 78s a man in his church had cut long ago. It was a religious record, but it was different. It was just whistling. I never heard nobody whistle like that. For thirteen minutes we heard the man in the choir whistle the immortal tunes. The last one wasn't religious. It was *Fur Elise*. He played it over and over. A wind came up and the house quivered. I was a little afraid. Although his eyes were wide open, he seemed asleep his lids half-closed like a cat's.

"Don't you like it on the water. We'll take the boat and go in to the tavern tonight. Maybe we will. I've got a bucket of crawdads to sell. This will pass, this will pass."

"Thank you for the food, Delainy. So, what happened next?"

"The man said he'd come to buy the painting."

"How had he heard of it?"

"I don't know. Maybe Larkspur."

"Didn't he get out of the boat?"

"Yes, just as I was passing water. The steam rose up off my piss."

"I know what you mean, pissing in the cold."

"The watch was cold as hell in the palm of my hand. I took the time. Fog blew past and there was moisture gathering underneath the facing."

"Where was your wife, and where was Sinda?"

"After she brought me the juice, she went to town. Sinda was off in the woods, dancing. I know because her leotards weren't hanging on the line with the sheets, and she'd promised her mother not to go to town with them on, anymore. Sinda. . . ."

". . . Sinda. Then what did the stranger do?"

"I said to him, 'Come into the light, stranger.'"

"What did he say?"

"He took off his black gloves. And I tell you I've never seen a sadder man, no man. On the way up the ladder into my house he stopped and put his heart — like this. One of his gloves dropped into the water. I helped him in, sat him down next to the stove. He drank all the whiskey he could, and always with his eyes on the painting — the one of Sinda. . . ."

"... Sinda."

"'My daughter,' I told him."

"Was he dying?"

"He told me, 'I would like to have this one, too.' A man so miserable. What should I say? It was cold, but he was sweating beneath his dark clothes. He smoked. He breathed rough. He looked at me, at the levels on my walls. He looked all around as if he couldn't wait to tell someone where he'd been. Before he left, he asked for one more drink. I poured a stout shot in his jar. He never smiled."

"Did he act like he was better than you?"

"No, he was like us."

"He was a good man?"

"When he asked for another drink, it was a like a last request."

"Did you sell to him? How much did he give you for them?"

"I don't know. I don't know if money changed hands. But as you can see, the paintings are gone."

"I saw them when I came in. I looked for them. If I knew where the man was I could take you there, and we could see them."

"Is that why you came?"

"Well, maybe Larkspur will become famous."

"You came for the money . . . I thought. . . ."

"It might be worth something to us all."

"But Larkspur is dead."

"But he can still be famous, still."

"Is that the way it is?"

"It came then, didn't it Delainy?"

"Yes. I imagine — I imagine it did. After I'd seen him off and his boat was gone, I went outside and took another leak. I looked up to the empty house. The sweet potato I had put in the jar the night before was sprouting like kudzu. There were bees in my room. But it was the wrong time of the year. And I could walk without the sticks. And there was a case of wine under my bed. The moon covered the dust in my house. That's when I saw it."

6.

HITCHCOCK'S TALE

Hitchcock's Tale

When I was fourteen years old I hit a man between the eyes with a pretty, smooth stone and killed him dead as hell. He'd shot one of Brother Yvo's deer. It was plain to see that the doe was thick in the sides with fawn. There was snow on the ground and the blood of three slain creatures. *Laudato sí, oa la morte secunda no farra male.* I put the man across my shoulders and walked back up the hill to the monastery.

It was a bright afternoon. As if Giotto had put a bluegill in a triptych. Yes, that afternoon, coming into the dark church with the sunperch windows. The monks were having their office. The old ones slept, and the young ones sang to keep warm. One of them was shivering, trying to play the recorder. They'd been singing all the while I killed the man in the field, I thought. My boots sounded like hooves on a wooden bridge when I walked up the aisle with the dead man over my shoulders. I threw the man down on the white linen of the altar, then I knelt down and cried out to them, asking them to hear my open confession. The younger ones came and held my hand and stroked my damp hair, and the farmer monks took the body away. I heard Brother Casimir, who was in charge of cleanliness of the grounds, tell the idiot novice to get a broom and sweep up the blood on the terrazzo floor. For awhile all I could see was spit: drooling out of the idiot's harelip, from the openings in the recorder, out of the mouths of the abbot and his acolytes; and there was the red spit of the doe and the dead man from town, and the invisible spit of the unborn fawn. It was a bright afternoon trying to swim upstream through the glass in the dark church.

The abbot and I, accompanied by Brother Yvo and some other young monks, rode mules to the courthouse. The abbot slept mostly on the ride, but Yvo went through his rosary of imagery for me: The hour, the darkness of morning, the constellations near death, the locomotive running by us with its fertilizer and hobos, dogs, the faces of schoolgirls walking towards the bus stop with their books, their legs soft as a cope. . . .

"Bless you, Brother Yvo, but that will be enough," the abbot said, swaying on the bareback of the big white mule. Like a wounded man, a drunk, a sleeper dreaming, the big abbot prayed for me.

The Judge said, "Son, you spent seven bad years in the orphan home, then the good brothers came for you, and since then you've spent a good seven years with them, but now this state requires you spend fourteen years and a day at hard labor in a sawdust camp."

The abbot gave me his blessing and the monks their kisses of peace. Then a greasy-headed man put irons on me, goosed me, and told me to hop in the back of a wagon with thirteen Negroes and two Creek Indians. A prisoner and a guard drove the wagon. Both of them had shotguns and pints of liquor in their hip pockets. I couldn't tell the trustee from The Law, I had no idea which was which: they both seemed to be sitting in judgment, waiting for judgment.

There was a horrible stench in the wagon, worse than the dead dogs we passed on the side of the road. In the late afternoon, after we were miles from town, we stopped under a large live oak near a wooden bridge. Honeysuckle was growing around it and it was good to breathe. The man who wasn't holding the reins turned towards us, handing me a large papersack full of cold biscuits and pointing towards the creek, and said, "We'll take a dinner and a water break now. Ya'll go ahead." He smiled and tapped the other one on the shoulder, "Say, Pentworth, I bet these boys want to catch up on a little shut-eye; I bet they about ready to work a little wood."

"Yes, Whumphead, I'm going to tell them what all the captain's got for them. Listen up you burr-headed, black-assed bastards. The captain he don't like nobody forgetting them trees. You know? So he fills up your mattress with leaves in the fall, and he puts sawdust in your pillow in the spring. The captain so nice, he going to give you a pretty comb and you better keep it clean. He going to give you a ax and you best keep it shining, you better keep it pretty, cause if you don't he going to turn you over to Tattoo Man, and Tattoo Man he part woman. He put a spider on your ass and an angel on your face." They both got a kick out of that.

Then he stuck a shotgun up to one of the Indian's head and said, "You stinking pig, if you can't squeeze enough whitehead grease out of your face to slick my gun, I'm going to cut you in two!" The Indian put the heel of his hand to his nose and pushed until his friend shook his head, trying to pull up the back of his shirt with his cuffed hands. He wiped off the little seeds of pus from his nose and then started pinching the swellings on his friend's back. The man on the wagon turned his attention to another young man who was fair looking, sick, and scared. Whumphead said, "Nigger, don't I know you?"

The young man was squeezing his small, white bible tightly, sweating down to his socks. He spoke up, "No suh."

"You positive?"

"Yes suh, I never been in this state before in my life. Until last week, and when I get out captain's logging camp, I swear I ain't never coming back."

"You mean you ain't got no kin in Arkansas?"

"I ain't got nobody here, captain."

"Don't you call me captain. They ain't but one captain. You call me Mr. Prince Albert. Got that?"

"I got it!"

"So you don't know nobody in this state?"

"Not a soul!"

Whumphead nodded at him and the young man smiled, opening his bible, peeking at something, smiling back again at the man with the shotgun.

"What you name," Whumphead asked him, pulling at the bill of his baseball cap.

"Sweet William call me."

"Well, Sweet William, since nobody around here knows you, I don't reckon you'd mind if I asked you to unhitch these mules and take them in the shade?"

"I be happy to do that, Mr. Prince Albert, I just be happy."

Sweet William unhitched them, and Pentworth told us to go lie down on the bridge and eat our dinner. "It's nice on the bridge. Ya'll can look at the water and I can look at you."

It was hot and dusty on the bridge. I heard a humming sound, like the drone of a chainsaw way off.

"Say there ain't a soul in Arkansas knows you, uh Sweet Billy?" The kid shook his head.

"Then take your pants off, you black son-of-a-bitch, and hop up on that stump and break a mule," he said, gritting his teeth and aiming the gun at Sweet William.

"I couldn't do that boss. I can't screw no mule. No suh." The man cocked the shotgun and shut one eye like he was aiming this time to shoot.

He took off his pants, looking back at us. They were held up by a piece of new rope. He clutched his bible, but a piece of paper fell out of it, a baseball card of Roberto Clemente fell in the dust. We could hear him breaking wind. He was the one smelling in the wagon. On the ride he'd told another he had the runs. It was some kind of worms he had. Partly from fear, partly from disease, we saw the bloody scours run down his legs.

"Goddamn you, Whumphead, you're spoiling my lunch. I got

some boiled eggs and tuna fish. The nigger's shitting like a calf."

A man in the middle of the bridge spoke up so no one but ourselves could hear him, "I kilt womens before, but not no white man. I'll get him. I ain't never coming out no camp a man anyway. They won't let Spiller out for nothing. I'll catch that hog some day. I'll tell him handle on my axe split. I'll get him close, then I'll split him like a rail. I'm going to get him bad. Ya'll watch Spiller, but don't be friends. I won't be long here, not long for this world."

"Shut your fucking mouths. Eat!"

"I'll eat it then, Pentworth. If you don't want it. When we get back to camp, you just verify my story. You just tell them Whump made a nigger shit all over his self."

"Get on the stump, Sweet Billy, hump the mule!"

"Nah suh, I can't Mr. Prince Albert."

"What you mean you can't?"

"I remember, I got kin in this state."

"You said you didn't, you better not be lying to me."

"Nah suh, I got me a Aunti in Mountain Home," he said, turning towards us, smiling, every now and then glancing down in the dust at the baseball card, while we stretched out on the boards of the bridge, eating the hard tack. It tasted like cotton.

"Ain't no colored people in Mountain Home!"

"I know. She white."

We all forced a laugh, trying to draw Pentworth to us and Whumphead away from Sweet William.

"Come on, Whumphead, let's do something else. Let's give these bastards something to think about," Pentworth said.

"Like what?"

"Like stir um up!"

"Let's get rid of one first. Hell, captain say not to bring back more than fifteen and we got sixteen here." When he said this even the men who hadn't budged before wiped the crumbs away from their lips.

"Alright, tell them."

"Wait a minute, hold on, look here what we got — we got a whop-nigger," he said, looking at me. "A young one. He can pass. Hey, kinkhead, how old are you?" I flashed five fingers three times, then took one away. The dumb monk had told me to pretend; he said they would rib me almost to death, but they wouldn't kill me. "You look old for your age, you good looking little dumbshit. Captain going to really take to you. I bet your pecker just. . . ."

"Listen up! How would one of ya'll feel if you knew somebody was sleeping on the floor on account of you? If somebody had to eat a half bowl of stew instead a full one. I'm doing you a favor. Think now. And after a long I said long — day's work. What about that empty bucket when you need a dip of ice water?"

A man near me, who'd said nothing along the way, spoke up, "They gone draw straws." "What you mean?" another asked him. "What I mean is one of us ain't gone wind up at the camp."

"Ya'll boys unzip your pants."

We lay down on the boards and put our members through the chink holes in the planks like they told us. Then Whumphead walked down to the creek and stood under the bridge. He took some smooth stones from the creekbed and threw them at the undersides of the bridge. We could hear the wasps getting stirred up. So it wasn't chainsaws I heard in the distance, I thought to myself.

The man next to me mumbled the name or a line from a song everytime he was stung. One man was preaching a sermon. I supposed it eased the pain. I remembered the chants of Brother Yvo: *Donna del paradiso, mi tengo a quest'albero mutilato abbandanato in questa dolina che ha il languore di un circo prima o dopo lo spettacolo e guardo il passaggio quieto delle nuvole sulla luna, questi sono i miei fiumi, sono un uomo ferito, regno sopra fantasmi, e nei vivi la strada dei defunti, siamo noi la fiumana d'ombre, che la mia vita mi pare una corolla di tenebre, e tu non saresti che un sogno, Dio, in noi sta e langue, piaga misteriosa.*

Some of the wasps came up through the spaces in the boards

and stung us over the eyes. We looked like prize fighters. The nests, we imagined, were big as sacks of oats.

It was getting dark. We shivered. "I guess we'll just pass the night here, boys," he said. The other one said, "Ya'll hung up in the bridge like she was a tight bitch."

They spread pallets in the back of the wagon. Bats flew under us, eating mosquitoes. Some of the mosquitoes ate us. To pass the time and pain, some of the men made up odd games. Someone pissed on a water moccasin. Someone said there was a nest of baby swallows near him, fluttering around next to his thing. Another said he hoped they had Moon Pies and soda at the camp, because he kept seeing the wrappers from town float by. We could hear catfish jumping below.

Later in the evening a wagonful of boys and girls on a church hayride came by. They halted on the other side of the bridge. Pentworth told the chaperones to make the boys and girls get out. Some of them were my age, and Sweet William's, and older. Pentworth crossed the bridge, took off his hat, and showed one of the chaperones a shallow place in the creek where they could cross. We heard the young people asking Pentworth why the prisoners were lying across the bridge. "Just security," Whumphead said. But before either of them could stop the young people, they were crossing under the bridge. One of them shined a flashlight up at us. "Ooh," the young girls moaned, holding onto the hands of their dates. The boys laughed, and the girls eventually turned their heads. A boy with a bow tie on, and without a date, told Whumphead, "Brother, don't you know that's not Christian!"

He whispered back to him, "Now don't you let the little ladies know, but all these here is rapists and murders. One of them used a hay baler on his wife. That's the truth."

The boy went, "Ooh."

The next morning a man on the end of the bridge said he heard a couple of the kids in the bushes. "They was in there all night. God knows what they was up to." I knew. The man said he heard the chaperone calling their names. I heard more than that.

Sweet William farted all night. He was the only one of us who didn't get up, the one who didn't go to prison. He got the shivers during the night. He told us he felt one of his guts explode inside like a mine. A man who had been in the service explained to us. He said it was his appendix; the fingernails collect there, like ants around sugar, and they probably cut his insides to ribbons. He got all infected. He was infected in the wagon on the way there. I could smell him then. Sweet Willy called out in the dark near the break of day that he was shitting himself to death. No one laughed. It wasn't funny. A man got his little, white bible and his baseball card. I think they did something to him with a knife — Whumphead and Pentworth — then rolled him off the bridge.

Back in the wagon a man said he saw a school of alligator gars go by. We passed a house with an old woman sitting on the front porch. The house was partially painted white, a new coat. We saw a fresh grave near there so we supposed her husband had passed away. There were daddy long-legs on the white part of the wall. Her yard was full of day lilies. She did not wave to us.

On the way a man went crazy. He reached behind his ear and found a little snail and started screaming. What was it that Yvo used to recite on the warm nights on the roof of the abbey: *Tutto ho perduto dell'infanzia e non potro mai piu smemorarmi in un grido.* I can no longer remember when the others pulled me out of bed by the ear, and the other orphans and I walked down those damp halls, half asleep, towards the large room filled with its many bowls of cold mush.

Before we got into camp they told us we better not try to run away. Pentworth rolled up his pant's leg and showed us a scar. So it was he. "Right here used to be a tendon or a ligament — whatever you call it. Not no more, though. The captain had his cook cut it out and fry it in a skillet like bacon. Didn't he Whumphead? He was in on it, boys! Then he made me eat it on a slice of toast with some soft-boiled eggs. I can't even run to the shithouse now."

"But don't get no notions cause he can still drop you. Tell um what they do the second time, Pentworth."

"There's a little midget with blonde hair named Speakeasy. He used to be a veterinarian. He's a real pal with the captain. Sometimes the boss invites him over for custard pie. They just love it. They sit there on the porch and drink ice water and eat pie until it's coming out their ears, and the captain asks him a favor, and little old Speakeasy says, 'Sure.' He still got some of those silver tools. He's got a little razor on one dull as everything. He'll cut you by God; he'll feed your nuts to the bloodhounds." Pentworth was taken over by an uncontrollable laughter and Whumphead had to shake him to make him shut up.

"Tell um what happens the last time."

"The last time—yea, I'll tell um. You black son-of-a-bitches, you go limping off with one nut and then get caught. Caught! The captain gives you to the preacher. He's a real fanatic. He's crazy as hell. He don't like soldiers or whores or pickpockets. He don't like it they nailed Jesus down on some two-by-fours and then let them thieves get off, strapped up and all and standing on buckets. So you want to know what he does? He takes you out to the woods where you been cutting lumber for the state. He makes you hewn out a couple of beams. Then you take a hand drill and bolt them together. He gets a sledge hammer and some railroad spikes and I mean he fastens you to the timber, like a buttonfly on a new pair of jeans. You yell, but ain't nobody coming. Not a soul in camp can sleep. Not even me and Whumphead. And if you pass out, the captain helps the midget up on the preacher's shoulders and Speakeasy he kind of chews on you. The damn dogs sleep at your feet with their mouths open. They waiting for something to drip—some of you. Listen, none of you bastards ever better fall in love!"

"We got everyone of you by the balls."

After seven years, during which time I often thought of the children in their beds and the monks in the fields, I received a pardon, with the provision that I should go into the service—the officers of the court and the local board pointed out that I would be entitled to seven years of higher learning under the G.I. Bill.

Aboard ship my dreams grew thicker than the weeds taking over the inner court of the abandoned abbey, and the past became like a dense thicket. I do not recall there ever being a woman. I see always, like a painting in which perspective has been deliberately diminished, Sweet William in the snow with a deer. Those days cutting timber for the captain of the mills; I learned how to whittle, how to protect my wrists, best of all — how to lie; I did not limp, I could function as a man, I never was nailed to a cross.

7.

ANSAR'S TALE
& LUPER'S NOTE

Ansar's Tale And Luper's Note

Where I come from strangers are welcome. They can sleep in the lofts, drink from the pumps, and use the outhouses. Like the dragonflies and the milksnakes and the chickenhawks, we are used to them.

One day a fisherman saw a stranger driving his truck down the levee. The fisherman knew he'd have to wind up at the crossroads. He tore out a page from his Bible that he kept in a plastic bag in his boat, and wrote a message on it. He tied it to the leg of one of his homing pigeons, and threw the bird up into the air and it flew over the water towards land. The message read: *HE DRIVES A CIRCUS TRUCK WITH BARS AROUND THE BED. DIDN'T SEE NO CRITTERS? BEWARE, ANYWAY. AS I PASSED BY SILO'S PLACE THIS MORNING, HIS MOTHER WAS READING HER HORROR SCOPE WITH A MAGNIFYING GLASS. SHE SHOOK HER HEAD WHEN I PASSED BY, WAVING ME ON. SHE SAID, "THERE IS A WARNING FOR STRANGERS." TELL SPILL THIS. WHATEVER YOU DO, BE SURE AND TELL SPILL.*

Was this a warning against some stranger, or in his behalf, I remember thinking. I wasn't sure of Silo's wording, and I didn't know what Mulligan would do after he read it. Others have said this was my first real introduction into the laws of: Semantics, Logic, Language, Astrology, Grammar, Theology, or whatever their field happened to be. But I know what the message said. I know because I just said what I said; and I know because I found it in an empty snuff can in Lemmual's outhouse.

That wasn't all I found. The two nails Lemmual was always claiming he was going to drive back down into the wood, the ones which had torn many pairs of trousers, were nailed into the side of the outhouse. A rock with blood on it was sitting on top of a well-worn book. The two nails had something pinned against the wood. The homing pigeon was still warm. The book was written by George Sand. There was no name on it, the cover had long been gone, but there was a note written on the first blank page after the picture of the strange looking woman. The note said: *TO ALL THOSE CONCERNED, LIFE IS FAKE ART.* Somebody going by O.W. wrote it.

On the way home I found another note written in the mud on the side of the ditch: *REALITY IS AN IMITATION OF ART.* The same O.W. did that, too. That evening Mulligan didn't come back home. Neither did Silo. The lantern in his boat stayed lit all night. I heard that a man heard the boat drifting in his sleep. That he woke up and walked down to the water in time to see it collide with a bottle floating on the water, then glide into the empty stall of his dock. That morning the others let loose the other bird in the straw cage. The posse followed it. There was a posse because I told them about the note and the rest in Lemmual's jake. They asked me did I leave everything lay like I found it. I said sure. I bet the men followed the bird for three days. It was odd where the bird took them, all over this half of the county. One man riding a horse found his wife in the arms of another, the school teacher found his best pupil with his eldest daughter. They found a man that loved rabbits. He got in a cage with them, naked. They found the real murder weapon in an old trial that would have set a woman free, had she not been stabbed to death serving her term. And they found two bus tickets to Paris, Arkansas and the room key to No. 9 in the Paradise Inn. The pigeon lighted down in more places, in more lives, than I can remember.

That sheriff wanted to know who O.W. was. I told him I didn't know his butt from a hole in the ground. I was almost done with the book, but the sheriff said I couldn't take it anywhere. He said it was admissible evidence, so I went to Lemmual's outhouse to read it.

Nature took its turn in the dark, but I arrived there long before sundown to read, as I had for several days. It was the last chapter, the last page, and in flew the homing pigeon through the stove pipe hole, and then one of the posse kicked in the door and they all looked at me with their guns drawn. I was drinking a Orange Crush.

One of the men was a state boy, I could tell by his uniform. He asked me a lot of questions. He said the folks around here are plumb strange. He said he'd never seen as many blind people in one spot on the earth in all his life. He said in our county a one-eyed man would be king. He asked me why there was so much blindness, so much sorrow. I told him I didn't know anything about any sorrow, but hadn't he ever been to a factory or a sawmill and seen workers missing fingers and things. It is the same around here, I told him, except nobody works hard at anything but looking, seeing, taking notice. So, they lose their eyes. He said that was some kind of occupational hazard. I said, no, it was just the way it was. He said a man would get rich selling glass eyes around here. I said, Mister, you see a big house up the road, he can't see out the window.

It was my first book I ever read clean through, I imagine. And I mourned for days for its passing; just like a bird mourning for its dead mate. They never found Mulligan, hide nor hair. Never found the stranger or Silo either, but I found another book. But let me tell you, I could have told them who he was, where he was holding up, but we made a deal. They never found him, though. They still got paper out on him. All the warrant says is O.W., and there is no face on the paper. I should have told them, but I wanted a book more than they needed their suspect. It was an exchange we made, the stranger and I. I never divulged his identity. He always laughed when I called him O.W. But how could I tell them who he was if he said he wasn't O.W. I only knew he left books in the outhouse. I forgave him all his cruelty in place of the books. I waited for them like a schoolboy waits for Friday afternoon. The dark house, with its wasps and odor, and I stared at the facing pages like woods I had never called or killed an animal in.

After my thesis was accepted, but the night before I actually received my Doctorate in Astronomy, I met with the Head of the Department and he told me, "Upon bestowal of this degree you know, of course, you will be the only black man in this country with a Phd. in Astronomy." I made the usual acknowledgment with a nod, the sort of ritual one goes through with the Head of the Department. He said nothing of my thesis, my years of study under him, or my research, nothing at all. But he did say something that night outside on his patio that bothered me then, and continued to work in my guts for several years thereafter. He said, "We have accepted your thesis only under the circumstances. We think it is the better thing to do; rather than withhold the degree, we will bestow it."

In a few years their benevolent act would make no difference, they would be spared the embarrassment of what they considered my ineptitude; all of their reservations could come to rest. My mother, whoever she was, had left me something, an ironic legacy for my field: syphilis. Little by little, my eyesight failed. The doctors were helpless. Finally, I went blind. The universe is a dark, starless outhouse now.

I live here in an old mansion leaning over the edge of the river. I can spit in the water from my backporch. Every year the water takes more and more of my bank away, until there is now not a slope to the river but a dirt cliff. I have a companion, a bright, young boy from across the river. Sometimes he brings his friend, a white boy. They both are at that age of constant awe. They both love the stars. Soon, they will love women. I let them use one of the upstairs rooms for their very own observatory. Together, when we can be, we read, and talk, and dream. Coose reminds me of myself at his age, accurate and quietly infatuated with everything. His friend, Luper, is a little mad. I fear what from. Perhaps I have more in common with him now.

We eat the evening meal together, and then we go out on the deck and I talk and they look at the heavens. After a lecture on terrestrial relationships, one night, Coose sighed and shook his head, while Luper kept on beating out a pattern on a pair of imaginary bongos, his eyes closed. Luper is more interested in bees and books than he is the stars. And I have them read to me in the daylight hours. I'm no longer interested in the professional journals, of course, only those books I read as a child, the ones I came to know in the outhouse, left by the stranger. I find both of these children, like myself at their age, completely unconscious of their thoughts and self-conscious of their actions. Yes, I have them read to me the likes of Sand, Wilder, Stevenson, Gide, Proust, Genet, Pirandello, De Maupassant, Wilde. From time to time I interrupt them with astronomical metaphors which lack any literary lineage whatsoever. I regress with allegories of my childhood. Still bitter over my position in space, I brood out loud, bemoaning my brief and uneventful scientific past. There were parties with learned men, I tell them, where "The grotesqueness of his childhood is beyond first magnitude," so sayeth the bossman, the Head Doctor of Astronomy. This was the sort of rape of innocence I detested. The adjective *grotesque*, when applied to my happy past like a bandage smelling of disinfectant, was far worse than *nigger* ever was. I thought *grotesque* was their learned way of calling me a jungle bunny.

Sulky and cunning, I began to paraphrase episodes from my favorite literatures for them, even passages from the Bible, interpreting them orally, as the boys watched on, wide-eyed I would suspect. As time went on, I suppose they thought me alien and hideous. My cornbread smelled like the stench of dead fish, my ears were full of worms. The children held me and gave me liquor when I shook. I heard Coose whisper to Luper during one of my spells, "It's awesome, man. He starts thinking about he can't see no more. No more moon, no more stars. Pain, man. Pain, pain. His mind gets out of focus." I heard them.

When I talk to them, especially at night, the bones protrude out of the architecture of my past, but their visibility is an integral part of the structure. Only now, when I can no longer perceive them, do I understand the nuances of perspective, and chiaroscuro in my childhood. My conception is still good, though I am not wise. I am mad. I am no longer in the light of wisdom. The universe has become dark and intentional. There is no longer any unpremeditation – not for me. Perhaps this is why I enjoy so much the company of Coose and Luper. They lack mechanics, they are like bullfrogs ready to catch sparrows. I am going mad and they know it.

I lack voltage. My memory is fading like a shirt in a men's store window. That is why I'm turning to literature. I plan to leave behind a book of essays dealing with the imagination. I plan to leave all my holdings to Coose and Luper. More and more, now, there are long, dark silences between what I say and what I mean. Yesterday, I told them about a grotto filled with butterflies. When, in fact, it was only the outhouse.

It takes awhile before I can relate with what I've just told. There are locomotives going by without sound. And what about that stranger, that bird, and the dark constellations of childhood.

In the movies, speeded action implied farce or ineptness. But slow motion does not always mean the deadly serious. Scenes flash by like a storm of meteors, obfuscating retention. Ansar is a thing of the past.

Bombarded with particles of knowledge, like dust on a mirror. How I buried my shoe with an apple core, the speed of light, the accidental discovery of the cinema dissolve, the age-old problem of *inspiration* in literature. Keats said, "My imagination is a monastery and I am its monk." Although Rossetti denied it, he was wise to Keats when he died. He knew the nova of chance. He knew monks live with chants. Keats, meditative stableboy, knew his limits.

The drizzle turns into rain. I am standing by the green river. There is a wrecked tugboat nearby. Coose and Luper are in the belly of the boat, telling stories. It is dark. They are looking for whatever they can find. They are not afraid. They have lanterns. But what of the stranger? Aloud, I recite the poem, "Light Breaks Where No Sun Shines." I am drinking whiskey, night fishing, and I cannot see the cork on the end of my line. I am thinking of what I can tell them today, no tomorrow. Perhaps there is some flaw in the making, some mistake entombed. Oh you watchboys tell me, what of the night, what of what you see. You have combed the hair of a blind man in the field of astronomy. There is a curious defect in man's perception. The architects of Greece knew this. They built a temple in which appears a mirage to cope with this. They knew how men's eyes refuse to see reality as it is. Color, scale, movement, three dimensionality were all forgone. I have a mansion leaning into the river. I have these two children for awhile. I have one night to dream.

Luper's Note

Ansar, the blind astronomer, was born here and came back to live here, took his own life many years ago. My best friend, Coose, is travelling through space at a phenomonal speed, heading towards a destination the government will not announce for years to come. He is the first black man in space. We write. Now and then.

Ansar might of told you I had a bad habit of reading, then making notes and putting them into empty bottles, and throwing them into the river. The river that flows along like a long, black moon. Well, those days are over. I live alone in Ansar's big house.

I sell bait for a living. And I put pilings up to keep the porch where it is. I am a poor fool, but I have many friends in the taverns and that part of the county no one will enter. As Ansar used to say, we were all figs of the imagination.

At night, when I dream in his bed, I remember. I write down what he says in these dreams. For example, "I am going to tell you about this woman, but first. . . ."

And I write, after him: What was natural is now abstract, singing pollywoddle doodle all day. Shadow, light, and color are parables. And dreams are deliberate. Atmospheric perspective is eliminated. The outhouse, the dead homing pigeon, the troth with the stranger. Take Giotto, the medieval painter and architect; he saw things different, like a monk sees a beautiful woman when he dreams, a woman who is not a virgin. Foreground, middleground, and background were no more. Form and color, like Ansar and the stranger, and Coose and myself, are symbols and allegory.

8.

THE FOOL'S TALE

The Fool's Tale

I came to know the honky-tonk angels like long lost cousins you meet at a Sunday School picnic. Boxcars, boathouses, plantations, whorehouses, monasteries, and barns. I was back in the old place again. Tyronza actually had a great grandfather buried seventeen feet from the Pentecost, Mississippi Catholic Church. The graveyard was throwing distance from the dive. You could drink beer and listen to Esrom dig holes in the ground.

Italian men, who had gone bad like their daughters, went across the gravel road to leak and cry. They crossed over the road, stumbling, like they were carrying a bullet not thirty extra pounds, to weep with their fathers. Buster Mascagni started out selling tamales and fudge his chair-ridden Mamma made. Now he's got a house the state senators chew matches over when he invites them over to his stands in deer season.

Buster's really something. One day he's clean, another he's filthy rich. He came in the bar one time with a cotton sack full of money. He's got a million bucks, a gin, one hell of a beautiful family, a prostrate the size of a musk melon, and credit clear over to Arkansas.

But the only way Buster can enter the state of Louisiana is if he's in a funeral entourage. It's better if he stays close to home, where everyone knows him. Whatever bad you can say about Buster Mascagni, he doesn't forget his friends, he never outgrew his trousers. He still goes to the same place to drink every Saturday evening after confession.

What I like, what I remember, are those guys that got lost, or the ones, the new ones, who come here just so they can go back and tell people where they've been. You can smell them a mile off. We've got a place out in the shade a ways from the building where we shoot it. Horseshoes, checkers, fish cleaning table, radio, records, dirty books, bait tank for our minnows and beer. In good weather, we sit out there lots. Every once and awhile a man from town, who doesn't want to confess to the other priest, comes out this way, looking for the church. We're sitting there, calling the shots, and some stranger asks, "Where is the good Father's rectory?"

"Why don't you go over to the *Creek*," we tell him.

"What creek is that?"

"Dick Creek's."

The priest is always over here in his old worn cassock, talking politics and crops and money. He can spin a tale like a cat. And I've seen him knock out troublemakers colder than a wedge. There's nothing like turning up in one of your old hometown haunts, with a little hard cash to go around. Spend it on those who need it, and pay back those who were good to you when you needed it, and play a little bones. There's no big shots where I come from. Picking up the tab, no big thing. Men here can make the buying of a round of drinks a mysterious gesture. I've seen men put their arms around one another on Saturday night, and cut each other down on Monday. There are signs that give a man away, letting you know when he's too mad and hurt to talk to. You don't want to slap a man on the back if he's stepping on the toe of his cowboy boot, trying to put something out like a match. And if there is a dead leaf on a strand of spider's web, floating like a kite, you don't want to cut in on a man if he's studying it. These boys are sensitive to the weather, like gardenias to the touch. And watch out for those men picking at ingrown hairs; when they get infected and they start thinking about their wife and who did it this time, keep your distance. They'll come down on you like a tree. I saw a man go crazy there once, at Creek's. He was looking at himself in the black table. It was raining outside, it had been raining to float chunks. I guess he'd lost all his beans; his soybeans. There's a chickenhawk that lives in the steeple of the church. He looked up and lightning hit that bird and rung the bell. He crumbled like dust, then swept himself up in a pile.

Under the counter, next to his pistol, Mr. Dick keeps a copy of the magazine I broke into print in. It's as shaggy and worn as a book of nasty pictures. "Ellis was always crazy and pulling things like that," Mr. Dick tells people when he gives them the copy of the magazine. That's my name, Ellis. Ellis Cinders.

The priest and Loudermilk are the only two men I had enough nerve to recite with. Father didn't look me in the eye and Loudermilk was hard of hearing so I really didn't mind. The first poem I ever got published got me in a little trouble back home. I used some real names and I had a few people coming down on me. When you do the number I did you get all sorts of people wanting to hang around with you. Crooks and cheerleaders you could go to jail for dating, even the scum of the earth drove up on Sunday afternoons and parked on the beach near our property and watched me walk up and down. I got to be pretty good friends with them, why else would I get run out of town? I did the whole bit, from Keats to the moon, to some down to earth bullshit. I made my coach cry.

The poem was dedicated to Ingmar Bergman. Maybe that's the reason they published it in the first place. You never can tell. They must have sent him a copy because he wrote back. "Thank you," is what he said, "I would like to see some more of your work." I like to think the poem gave him a few ideas. I carry his letter, envelope and all, wadded up in my wallet like a schoolboy's rubber. I like to take it out and read it before I go to bed. I guess it was on account of the letter that I ditched my wife and kid. Well, she really wasn't my wife, and she wasn't really my kid. My real wife got stabbed six hours after we were married in Transylvania, Louisiana. She was fourteen and I was thirteen. We left the church in a boat on the swamp. She was holding roses and a candle. It was the acolyte who killed her.

At the bottom of the letter he said, "You are somewhere in between Robert Burns and James Cagney." That really hurt my feelings. I got around to sending him some more stuff like he asked. I expected to get a long letter, but all I got was a post card saying he was eating yogurt, fishing, and listening to his child play Hugo Wolf. There was something else, though; but I misread it, and I won't say what he really said, only what I thought he said. "Would you like to write a film about Emily Dickinson? Use Ingrid Thulin with dark hair. What do you say?"

So, I left home. I left the city where I was obscure as Orion's dog in the city, left my family of sorts, and wrote this screenplay I thought Ingmar Bergman directed me to.

I moved into an old home in the country. It was all grown over. All the folks around here think it's haunted, so nobody comes to visit, only the priest, Loudermilk, and Buster Mascagni. There is something sexual in all the vines and mystery surrounding the place, like the inside of a flower. Cold moonlight, a circle of stones in the window. The wasp nests were so thick it took a snow shovel and a drum of gasoline to get rid of them. They say the old owner came back to look at his place many years ago. The wasps stung him to death. I guess I believe in things like that. Emily speaks of ourself behind ourself, the rare life hidden in silence; she says she cannot live with her lover because it would be life. She believes in all that dust, just like me; just like I believe Jesus felt his blood running down his toes, and was so crazy he could believe he did such a thing just for me. It's the dreams I thought Bergman wanted.

When I was a kid I thought we were getting a new Catalog in the wrong time of year. It turned out to be a collection of Symbolist painters, sent to the wrong address. I kept the book, hid it so nobody would send it back. They found out, though. I put my cousin's eye out for tearing a page out of the book, and I killed the dog that pissed on it. One of those painters said Christ was poet, how else could he believe all that. Who else would have an imagination like that; only a fool.

I froze my ass off many nights writing scenes for Miss Emily, gash of shadows, still young, dying to make love, sitting at a french desk, shawl around her, soiled doilies, and always a rose in an urn for her to prick her finger with. This anchoress always had her thumb on a thorn, like a button. I dreamed her dreaming a close-up of her clitoris, slipping around in something soft and dark like the eye of a buzzard. I even went to town and put stockings on so I could take them off on a street at night and write the scene.

I would see her cutting back the roses in the hours before dawn. At my desk, I would see her in the undergrowth, hear her climbing the stairs, watch her, partially hidden by the canopy, enter my bedroom. And then it would be me going into her room. I would be going into Miss Emily's bedroom. I worked and worked the ore of my dreams until it was a fine radium. I had it all ready to mail one Friday afternoon when a kid comes riding by on a bicycle. He rides past the mailbox where I'd scribbled my name. He bears down the whole weight of his body on the left pedal, fishtailing over the dusty road. He turns around and heads up to the front door. He's too short for the knocker, so he just kicks it open.

Here was this kid with a note pinned to his coat. "You don't know who this is. All of us read your poem. It was nice. This is your son. The doctors say he's autistic. At first I thought they were saying artistic. None of us can handle him. I've had it up to here. You take him. He's strange. Your childhood sweetheart and secret admirer." No name was given.

"You wanna fight?" were the kids first words, "Or you want me to play the piano?"

Wait until I told Dick Creek, the priest, Loudermilk, Buster Mascagni, and Ingmar Bergman. He jumped up on top of the white piano and said, "I have a green belt in karate and I can play anything that moves."

9.

MERTON'S TALE

Merton's Tale

Lieder eines fahrenden Gesellen.

The bells tolled two. I woke, washed my face in the bowl of water beside my bed, put on the clothes, packed a bag I could carry over my shoulder, and left. It was dark and cold. A thin sheet had glazed over my bowl and around my window. My breath rose upwards with the clouds passing in front of the moon. My wool pants and dark sweater smelled like the tobacco I kept hidden in my closet. The black overcoat was too large, but it was warm.

It was a four mile walk on the frozen dirt road to the highway. When I got there, I built a fire to take the chill out of my bones, and to flag down the bus. The only thing I owned of any value was a pocketsized tape recorder, and a small collection of classical music. As I waited, I took the recorder out and set it on the end of the long log in the fire. One end wasn't burning. I leaned against it. It played by itself, but I feared the batteries about dead. It looked like a turtle on the end of the log. When I was a child they said if a turtle ever had you between his jaws, it wouldn't let go until it thundered.

The bus pulled up in the cold fog like a ship running contraband. I boarded it and took a seat near the back, consciously avoiding the faces of the other passengers.

Dark snow fell, as if here and there along the road hidden

hunters were blasting into the breasts of doves. The man driving came over the loudspeaker above each seat, "This is the voice of your driver, John Robbins, who's been driving these routes going on ten years. Lay back and dream, folks, I'll get you to where you are going. But if it keeps this up outside, I'm not sure if we'll reach our destination or not. I don't even know if we'll make it to the next rest stop. If any of you aboard has a transistor radio, please tune in to the nearest station and try to get the weather. For those of you who are awake, we will soon be crossing the Lake of the Algonquins, and approaching Mt. Nebo. Thank you for your attention. And a pleasant journey. This has been your driver, John Robbins."

Das Lied von der Erde

The ice held us on top of the mountain. We were stranded all during the light hours, but by nightfall the roads had been cleared and we were travelling again. During that time, I became friends with a group of Indians who used the buses to wander. They had wine and a sack of jellybeans and candy apples left over from Halloween. I drank and ate with them. They listened to my music, but they liked country music on the radio better. We sang and told dirty jokes. They kept asking me would I like some old chicken they had in a papersack, but I always turned them down. The wings and gizzards and thighs seemed to replace themselves. Although they looked and talked like bums, they were considered by their tribe a chosen people. They had been chosen to wander, searching and roaming all their lives for the lost graves of their ancestors. It was a belief in their tribe that until the graves were properly attended, the souls would remain lost forever. They were also searching for someone who lived, called The Dark One in their mythology. I pictured a tall, lean, Greek-looking hero, but I was taken aback by the old, wooden painting the large Indian woman showed me. The god, who was also a man, was short and stout with a low, protruding forehead. His hair wasn't long and smooth and straight, but gnarled. He had a face ugly as sin. She slapped me on the knee and said something about his sexual prowess that made me blush. Her name was Turkey Who Sleeps All Day On The Chinquapin. An Indian sitting in the back of me kept leaning over and whispering in my ear, "You better watch Turkey Woman. She has big, thick, greasy lips like you know what," and he laughed until she hit him with whatever she had. She drank more than the men, and ate Divinity they had picked up at resting places all across the country. "The Dark One is a bad ass," she told me. "He might cut our throats and drink our blood."

There was a legend to The Dark One but they wouldn't tell me the whole thing. Parts of it were sacred, and could only be told to members of their tribe. They had a strange kind of reverence for him; I'd seen it before by others for other gods. "He has green eyes and his hair don't blow like a pony mane, it blows like owl feathers," Charlie Firebuilder said.

Walking down the road to catch the bus something flew in my eye out of the night air. A speck of dust, perhaps. I tried to work it out during the bus trip but it was lodged in well. The Indians said that if it bothered me more than a couple of days it just wasn't any speck, it was a piece of star. Charlie Firebuilder said that when he was a boy some starlight came down and seeped into his eyes.

Symphony No. 1, The Titan
Symphony No. 5, The Giant
Symphony No. 7, The Song Of The Night

Going down the mountain was dangerous. We slipped from the road like a fish from a girl's palm. When we reached the little Town Of The Springs, the driver said it was as far as we would be able to go that night. We would have to layover until the bad weather passed. The bus company would put us all up in suitable lodgings. "Bout time, man is plumb crazy driving on ice in the dark," Turkey Woman said, gathering up her belongings, which included a hair dryer and a tiny color T.V. set.

We weren't the only ones stranded for the night. Most of the motels and inns in the tourist trap town were filled. The ice storm had covered a large area and many travellers had to wait in the small town. The Vacancy signs were lit with No. The village was laid out in steep hills, and the roads were narrow and curving. The bus driver was trying to calm everyone down in the service station which was also used as the Line's waystop. He told everyone some way or another they'd all get put up for the night, and everyone would get a fine meal. He was calling all around on the phone. While the other passengers went over the faded city map tacked to the service station wall, the Indians carefully examined the worn maps they had in a sack. The maps were on wood and leather. I took a state map from a stack under the counter and compared it with their old drawings, full of symbols and signs. I was amazed at how close the old Indian maps were to the more recent state maps; the natural monuments like bluffs and rivers and hills and lakes all scaled out. The Indians had even had a way of plotting topography. "Turkey Woman," Charlie said, "this is holy place we're at. Magic water flow here. Man wash himself and have many sons. Woman drink and can work long days. Get phone book and see if we got kin here."

The streets wound back and forth, up and down; the buildings were an odd mixture of gothic, Victorian, Swiss, and hillbilly design. They weren't built by sane men. They were built *into* the steep sides of the hills, not on them. We were put up in a peculiar edifice, The New Tara Hotel, a leaning firetrap of a place. The other passengers lucked out and stayed in the newer motels at the edge of town. I guess people thought the little earphone coming from the inside of my coat was a hearing aid and not the cord to my tape player, because they always animated their speech, talking very loud. I didn't think twice about leaving the others and going with the Indians to The New Tara, just considered it luck, but Turkey Woman said, "They put us here on purpose."

The old woman who gave us the pen to sign our names pounded the bell on the desk, but the black man in the fez, sitting near the huge, drooping fern, smoking a cigar and looking at the late movie, didn't get up until there was a commercial. I could see that he was missing an arm. "Rosemont will show you to your rooms," the old woman said, grimacing at him.

Something was still in my eye, it wouldn't budge, not even with tears or constant picking. I tried to wash it out in the water fountain in the lobby of the hotel.

I recognized the old movie as *The Big Sleep*. Rosemont picked up my bag, but didn't consider touching the luggage belonging to the Indians. He stood still, holding my bag, his eyes glued to the set. Then he set it down. "Go on, Rosemont," the old lady called out. He picked it up again and walked towards the stairs. "I can get this, go on and watch your program," I told him, taking my sack. The old woman was reading the names we wrote in the register with a magnifying glass. She looked full of consternation.

The elevator had an out of order sign on it, but I saw it come down and a man in a wheel chair rolled out, started to speak, but the woman behind the desk said, "No, Mr. Laughton, the checks haven't come for this month yet." I saw the black man motion the other old gentleman over his way, opening his coat and pointing to the neck of a bottle inside. The man wheeled himself over to the porter and I could see them trying to hide something from the old woman. We walked up several flights to our rooms, carrying our own light luggage. I could see shapes of light change on the floor as we walked by the cracked doors. Then the latches closed. "Some Hotel," Turkey Woman said. "Ring the bell tonight for a bottle of wine, and some old one-armed niggerman show up tomorrow morning with a pot of bitter coffee when I'm using the bathroom. Charlie, let's do some calling and see if we got kin here." "One-armed man didn't get luggage," Charlie Firebuilder said. All of us found our rooms and said goodnight. As I was walking down the hall to mine, the door to a room opened quietly by itself in the draft; it was a small, dimly lit room, sunset colored. A young girl was lying nude on the bed. Her eyes were wide open, so wide she seemed to be in a trance. An older man with silver grey hair was kneeling next to her, his face on her pale belly. He heard me and looked up, startled. I stared at the girl. "Shut the door nurse," he shouted, pulling out the knot in his tie. And a woman in white closed the door.

Symphony No. 6, Fate
Symphony No. 8, The Thousand
Symhony No. 4

They went to sleep, but I could not. From my window I noticed shining near the Hotel a six pointed star. It was the light over *The Star of David Tavern*. I walked out on the cold, windy gallery — what most people call a balcony — where the icicles hung down like knives, threatening, I thought, the pedestrians below. And on the other side of the narrow street I saw a tall woman in a long, hooded coat walking slowly and carefully over the ice. She was carrying a baby, passing in front of the lit window of a closed shop. She looked in the window, using it for a mirror. She looked around, covered the child's face with the blanket, and reached into her pockets. She drew out a handful of soda crackers and began tearing off the wrappers and eating them. She must have eaten ten or twelve packages in the shop foyer. The old sign of the Hotel creaking on its hinges made her raise her eyes. I think she saw me, but I think she did not want to let me know. She stuffed a cracker back into her pocket and walked on up the winding hill, once almost falling with the baby. The speck in my eye burned like a grain of sand.

The bartender was a big man with a black beard. He looked like a sailor and he spoke with a bad lisp. It was warm in the tavern and I drank the beers fast. I hadn't been there a half hour when in comes someone and tells the bartender, "The Schindler girl died an hour ago up at the Hotel."

It was dark in the tavern, but I could see stuffed fish on the wall, a headdress, a painting of a woman and a child washing in the river, a dime-a-ride pony with a boy on his back, a table where men played dominoes, a table where two women played snooker, some arm wrestlers, a man working on the juke box with a screwdriver, and a whole family crammed into a booth making signs with their hands. I asked the bartender about them and he explained they were all deaf and dumb. For a living they hauled firewood and trash. The boy on the pony belonged to them. He was motioning for a dime but they had none. He saw me looking at him, then he got off the hobby horse and walked over to me at the bar. I gave him a dime. Then his sister came over. The younger the children, the prettier they were. All of them over sixteen or so lost their features. She pointed to a jar of beef jerky and held out her hand. The bartender told her, "Shoo," and cracked a towel at her. She jumped back but I caught her, handing her several dimes. One of the older children came over, grabbed her by the wrist and twisted until she gave him some money. He bought a beer with it. I took several sticks of jerky out of the jar and gave them to her. I smiled at her efforts trying to chew it. But she thought I was laughing at her. I hadn't noticed she was without teeth; she was so young. No older than the girl in the Hotel.

Two good looking gentlemen were sitting in the corner, one of which was looking at me. He held up his glass, as if offering me a seat. The bartender spoke under the cuff, "Listen, this beer here is on that guy over there in the corner, the one with the moustache and pretty scarf. Beware of him. He's nice looking, but strange and dangerous. They call him Wicked Dick Turner." I took the beer, turned on the stool, acknowledged the drink, and the one he called Dick Turner half smiled at me, his eyes partially closed.

The little girl I gave the change and jerky to was sitting on a log near the wood stove. She was weeping. I imagined she was in a movie with no sound. The show in the hotel was the first movie I'd seen in a long time. I'd forgotten how easy it was to be held under their spell. A little drunk, but feeling no guilt, I walked over to her. I brushed her dirty bangs off her forehead. She smiled. I touched my teeth and made the sign for pain by poking myself in the heart with an imaginary knife. She nodded. I opened my mouth. She was a little hesitant, then she did the same. I felt her gums and she flinched. They were soft and pink, but the dark parts were infected. A dentist could perform a little surgery, get down into the rotten roots, and put on white caps. She would look lovely. I took out a pencil and I meant to write it down on the beer napkin for her, but she took the earphone out of my ear, put it in hers, then I saw her older sisters and brothers, their twisted faces. All I wrote down was *What is your name? Celia* she wrote. *My big brother says I have to get five bucks but I can do it with you for nothing.*

Dick Turner was standing over us. The girl leered at him and left. I wadded up the paper and tried to squeeze what she'd written away. "You need another drink, pilgrim," he said. He must have noticed the expression the deaf and dumb girl left on my face when he said, "Sorry. We call every stranger pilgrim here. No harm." I smiled, thanking him for the beers, shaking my head. For whatever the bartender had told me about his reputation, he seemed amiable enough. He held out his hand, inhaled on his cigarette, and said, "Dick Turner." I shook hands with him. He seemed to sway, as if he were holding his damp, luminous eyes in their place in his head. "What, no name?" he questioned. "I'd rather not; just yet," I said. "Care to join us — I can call you pilgrim now, since you won't give me a name," he asked, laughing. "No. No thank you," I said. Rather than a first conversation, I felt as if he and I were reciting something. Then the ice broke.

"I've had a long, cold journey, and this fire feels nice," I said.
"You like fire?" he asked.

"When I'm cold."

"Look out the window," he said. "Do you see those blue lights on top of that hill? That is my house. It is the house of pleasure. They call me Wicked Dick Turner, but listen. That house is pure, just like the water that comes from these healing springs. Have you bathed in them yet? You must before you leave. I have books, music, women, hashish, paintings to order – depicting those things every man dreams, good liquor I have made in the hills, did I say music?"

"I have music."

"Oh, is that music? I thought you were deaf, reading my lips. I'll speak faster and lower. Funny how we raise our voices to those who can't hear."

"Thank you for the beer."

"Come with me, friend. Look over there where I was sitting. See him. He can go with us if you like. And those women shooting pool. Come with me, just one night."

"Not tonight."

He undid the piece of rawhide holding his hair together, then he shook his head so that his black waves fell over his face and shoulders onto his tweed jacket, some of it touching the back of my hand. "Come to my house, pilgrim, come tomorrow night."

"I'm just passing through, stranded here with the weather. I have no desire to do anything but wait, stay in my hotel alone, and wait until we leave."

"I see," he said.

I motioned the bartender to bring us a round. And it was as if my arm was a direction to the tall woman in the long, black coat to walk by with her child. I stared at her, a woman walking alone over the ice with a baby, it snowing outside, it being late and dark and cold.

He saw me looking at her. "Friend," he said. "This town is different, don't you think? We have many tourists. Is there anything about any place, anyone you wish to know? I can tell you everything about everyone here." He waved his arm over the room.

His eyes lit up, opened wider, when I asked him, "Is she . . . a . . . what can you tell me about her," as she walked in, walking towards the stove, towards us, then seeing us, recognizing me from the gallery and then deciding not to warm the child and herself there. I rubbed my eye; it felt like a rising, not an eye.

"I can tell you a few things, I hear things, but I'm no crystal ball. I leave that up to the gypsies and Indians."

The baby was strapped on her back like a papoose. She took off her gloves, blew on her hands, looked over at the stove, mad it seemed that we had taken her place. The bartender brought her a quart and helped her take the baby off her back. She did not pay. He laughed and poked at the child. She was dressed in overalls, cowboy boots, and a white sweater; I could see when she took off her coat. She was pale and shivering, a bit overweight. The baby couldn't have been over a few months old.

"She's not married. She's a painter. She's mean. An alcoholic. Very little money, but will take nothing, only a beer from Jim up there. And since the child, she's not only mean, she's grown bitter. She must think she's vulnerable, so she's resentful. Proud, sardonic, in general a bitch and a loner. She's big. Knocked a guy out once. Some say she's sweet on women. I know a few women up at my place that have the hots for her. Never see her with men, so I don't know if she likes them or not. I'd say yes. Too bad. You're not the first I've told about her, the first to ask. A lot of men are attracted to her. Before the baby was born, I think many of the local men were afraid of her. I told you I knew everything. So why don't you forget about her and come on up to my place? See it up there on the hill?"

"What is her name?"

"Her name . . . Annie."

"Annie who?"

"Annie is good enough. A few people call her Mary, or Mary Ann. What difference does it make? Is that what you want, stranger? You want to meet her?"

But I wasn't listening to him anymore; I was watching her

Merton's Tale 71

sketch the deaf and dumb children on the beer napkins. Each of them was taking turns holding the baby.

"Jesus Christ, doesn't anyone have a radio," the bartender shouted. "Some son-of-a-bitch plugged up the juke box with slugs again!"

The deaf and dumb girl, who had read his lips, pointed towards me. There was a silence. Everyone in the bar looked at me, waiting for me to do something. She outlined a small square with her hands in the air and pointed under my coat, reaching in about my waist. I pushed her hand away, looking around the room. My eye felt as if it were about to break open like an egg. They must have thought I had a radio.

"Friend," the bartender called out, "I'm buying you a drink, but we're all waiting on you for music!"

I felt very self-conscious. "This . . . a . . . this is not a radio, but a tape recorder, it only plays tapes, nothing else. It can't run on any other power but its own, and I think the batteries are about dead," I said, hoping to quiet them.

"Give her a try!" the bartender yelled, opening a few more beers. "It's cold as hell out there and we need some music!"

"I don't know if you would care for my kind of music," I said.

"Listen to that, his kind of music, the pilgrim says," the bartender laughed, throwing up his arms. "Brother, we love it all. Let's hear *your* kind of music."

"Well, alright, but I'm warning you," I barely said, looking down and then at the girl called Annie.

Dick Turner reached in his coat and gave me one of his cards, "If I can be of any help while you are here, let me know." It gave his address and said he sold exotic plants and herbs. Saying, "Good evening," he got up and left, returning to his friend at the other table way off in the corner.

Everyone stared at me, waiting; everyone but Annie, who was looking out in the night, the snow, and her face in the glass. She put her hands through her hair, leaning on one arm. Automatically,

I slipped my hand inside my coat, turned up the volume, and pulled out the cord so all could hear the cartridge I'd put in. I watched her play with her silver, all over her hands, around her neck, and in her ears. She must have made them herself. The fire was hot enough to make me doze; it had been a long day. If this is how it is, still, I thought, if I must be laughed at, then I want to be asleep, listening to them then.

Kindertotenlieder

    I heard the racket of the cue balls again, the sounds of tight men betting, and beer being ordered; I knew they wouldn't like the music. Someone had come during my brief nap and turned down the volume. Now, as only I listened, the deaf and dumb girl looked in my eyes, as if she were feeling what I was. But Annie did not look at me, and I did not look at her, as should be. The clock said it was late, and someone had fixed the juke box. I told the girl goodbye, got up and I left, I think, unnoticed.
    The snow had quit falling, so I walked through the steep streets to sober up. On the hill, I could see the blue lights of his house almost in the clouds. I passed the shops: antiques, dulcimers, herbs and teas, gems, books, baked goods, ladies' wear, arts and crafts, then the picture window of a small gallery in which sat an antique trunk, the lid opened and suspended by golden chains. It was full of silver jewelry. Some of it was trite, some of it fine. It was called The Lost Springs Gallery, named so, according to an old plaque, because of a spring which ran underground not twelve feet from the building. The jewelry looked familiar. The legend said a holy man from the Algonquin tribe drank the water from the spring and washed his wounds; he saw a woman and followed her and was never heard of again. All of the other springs had been traced; they knew where they began and where they ended. This one disappeared.
    The steam from the warm springs rose all around me like the

breath of some animal sleeping underground. The entire town was full of these little springs and legends. I tried to look back into the gallery at the paintings, but it was too dark. There was only one light on the chest. It looked like the den of a pirate. I made my way over the ice, without falling, walking up and down strange streets, drinking from every spring I came to, listening to the wind chimes on the elaborate porches, looking at the ferns in the windows of the many oriels, listening to my music.

Charlie woke me up the next morning. I couldn't have been asleep that long. "Just wanted to check in on you, Turkey Woman was worried about you. Listen, I've been out to drink magic water. It is good for the ailments. It is good for the tired eyes. And it is good with whiskey. Here, I'm leaving a jar of it next to the foot of the bed. Turkey Woman blessed it. Go back to sleep now. The bus won't be leaving today, I already checked. Sleep."

When I woke again it was dark and a sadness hovered over my small room like an angel. In the next room over I could hear a voice, someone rocking and humming, an old person, I thought. I had high hopes for an afternoon with Charlie, Turkey Woman, the older porter and the other guests held over. I thought of going to the package store and the bakery and we could all have a get-together in the lobby. Instead, the day, another one, had gone. And there was a note under my door. "Found kinfolks. Bill Nestfinder and his family live on mountain near here. So we going to go, me and the Turkey Woman and the rest. Sorry to leave without speaking to you, friend. We going to watch it on the roads. Did you hear about the accident? So long, brother. Charles Firebuilder."

New friends leaving suddenly are like the holidays when your relatives come to visit for just one day. Perhaps you haven't seen some of them since childhood, but they always go back to those they haven't seen since last summer to spend their good times.

It would be the bar again tonight, I thought. Out the window I could see more snow falling. I missed the Indians already. There would be more stranded guests, I hoped. But downstairs there was no one, not even the one-armed porter.

I looked in the cabinet where the keys and registration cards were kept. Only a night there, I was already anxious for others. I sat down near the fern, smoked my pipe, and watched the townsfolk go by. Some more travellers checked in. I had hoped to speak to them but they were off to eat. The old woman left. I saw a card next to mine in the cabinet. I got up to go peek, but the old man in the wheelchair appeared, asking, "Have the checks come?" He told me his room number. There was an envelope but no mail. I handed it to him. "My rent is due," he sighed, wheeling himself back to wherever he'd come from.

A girl came in with a warm sack from the bakery next door. We nodded at one another. She took off her mittens, tam, and scarf, and sat down near me. They were brownies she was eating. I hadn't smelled a brownie in years. "Pardon, but is the bakery still open?"

"No, just closed."

I think she could tell I was hungry. She handed me one. "Thank you."

"That's o.k. You staying here?"

"Yes. Last night and tonight."

"Me too. Isn't this weather something? An ice storm here, I still can't believe it. Do you have the time?"

"I don't have a watch."

"It doesn't make any difference."

We talked for an hour or so, then she pulled out a deck of cards from her purse. "You know how to play Hearts?" she asked me. I told her I'd try. We played until the young man she was waiting for arrived. She got her key out of the cabinet and I noticed it came from the slot next to mine.

I wasn't hungry anymore, and it was still too early to go to the tavern. The streets were getting treacherous just to walk on. I waited for anyone to come down; the porter, the man in the wheelchair, the old woman behind the desk. I found a book but it was too dark in the lobby to read, so I went back to my room. I lay on the bed, listened to the pigeons coo and tried to read. I kept thinking about the young girl, the dead girl I saw on the bed. She didn't look like she was dead, she looked as if she'd been bathing and had seen something, had some vision. My eye ached. Then I heard her voice. The girl I'd just met downstairs. It was as if there was no wall to the next room. I heard them undressing, the boy taking off his pants, the girl throwing her sweater across the room to the floor; she laughed. Then there was the sound of something sheer, fabric sticking to the bedspread, her hose making an electric sound, like static, or webs in your hair when you walk through the forest. I had no right to listen. I put the earphone in and shut my eyes. Once again that sadness set in like an infection.

Lieder aus Des Knaben Wundrhorn

    I dreamed I was rich and free. I was a wealthy eccentric who used his palatial dwelling for a home for wayward girls. I ran an orphanage like an exclusive school. There were no broken hearts, no terrible rules. And there were many small children, the sons and daughters of the girls. Charlie Firebuilder was the professor of graces and Turkey Woman was an aged primadonna. The one-armed porter's only duties were to tell long stories. Annie, the woman I'd seen walking through the icy streets, taught art. She was something of a governess, the favorite of the girls. She held her classes out of doors in the gardens. Every afternoon I drank wine in a room full of sunlight and mirrors, and the room smelled of baby powder, dancers' talc, and the sweat of young girls. Every day they wore different colored leotards. Their hips were like loaves of bread.

    One day I sat in a beautiful chair in Turkey Woman's classroom; smoke drifted up into the dance floor. The lessons continued. Then down the hall I heard the steps of running children.

The deaf and dumb girl burst into the room, crying. She said there had been a fire in the museum, and all of Mistress Annie's paintings had been burned. And so had Rosemont. He went into the blaze to get the paintings. Then Charlie went in after him. He was still in there, she said to Turkey Woman with her hands. All the young dancers were huddled around Turkey Woman, all except for the dead girl. She was staring out the window, and then she sang an aria. There was the sound of Mistress Annie's sobbing, of exhausted dancers, and the shout of a girl moving across the slick floor with a splinter in her foot, which was the girl in the next room, and I woke up.

On my way to the tavern I slipped. Had it not been for the baker I would have slid all the way down the hill and off the side. "It's mean tonight, and going to get worse. Did you hear about the accident?" he said, helping me up.

"No. What happened," I said, helping him pick up the bread he had spilled on the ground, most of it having rolled down the hill.

"The Gaylord family were on their way up to Lost Spring Mountain to Dick Turner's place, you know, to get the trash. They had all the kids in the back of the pick-up. You know who I'm talking about, those deaf and dumb kids. Slid right off the mountain. They found one of the little ones down in Lost Spring, plumb froze to death."

"The family of mutes in the bar you say?"

"Yes, them."

Symphony No. 2, The Resurrection
Symphony No. 9

I drank until the bartender closed the tavern. I said nothing to anyone, only asking for more beers. There was an old picture of Louis Armstrong in a soldier's uniform, holding his horn. I scribbled *Etenium se incet incertam vocem tuba det, quis apparabitur ad bellum?* on the table with my finger. "Time to shut up now," Jim said, helping me out the door and putting several bottles in the deep pockets of my overcoat. "Right up there is your hotel. Just walk straight up the hill and cross the street and you'll make it o.k.," he said, thinking I was drunker than I was.

But I passed by my motel, walked past the porter and the man in the wheelchair drinking themselves and smoking cigars and laughing and watching the late show. I could see them through the window. I knew where I was going, up the street to Lost Spring, to Annie's gallery.

Symphony No. 3

It was dark, as if no one had been there since I'd last looked in the window, so I still couldn't see the paintings. Across the road, the cave and the spring formed a kind of grotto. The cold blood of the moon shone on the blades of ice. It was smooth and hard. The deaf and dumb girl was dead, I thought. My eye was rotting. Something came out of the sky.

There was a sound like bones cracking. I could barely open my eyes. From a large window, I saw the sun coming through the ice, melting it. I looked to my right in the room, and there was Annie, a pin in her mouth, and a diaper full of shit in her hand. I felt something like needles going under my toenails. The foot of the bed faced the window. It was almost too bright to see. I could feel something chewing my toes; there was something on the floor, like a dog. When I tried to speak there was a sharp pain in my head. Annie put her finger to her lips. "Don't speak." She changed the baby. Now my foot was tickling. My laughter cut into the back of my mind. I grimaced so hard I thought I would crush my eyes.

"You passed out at the mouth of the cave, where the little Gaylord girl was found. Dick Turner and I found you, but you didn't want anything to do with us. You said you had to go back, you kept saying you had to return. You were frozen up like the spring in the cave. The music on your tape recorder was going."

"My feet feel like they're frostbitten."

"No, that's Naima Nykvist biting your toes. She's Swedish. She lives in the apartment above me."

The old woman looked like a witch. Her scarf was ragged and she wore a black patch. She had on rubber boots, which covered up her short, swollen legs. Her rear was too large for the wool skirt she had pinned in place. She sucked on my toes as if they were candy or roots. "A good, strong flow of the blood," I thought I heard her say. "And he smells like goat. Naima's been kneading him like bread all night and morning, so Naima's got to go and see how Rosemont is doing."

The old woman, who was kinder than she looked, pinched the baby's cheeks and left. Her gnarled fingers had nails that rounded over the ends like lima beans. "Thank you," I nodded.

"Now tell me what happened."

"After Dick walked me home, he stopped by the cave and invited you up to his place. We were both worried about you. But you told him you were going back to the hotel. He left. I watched you talk to the stone owl. You were so drunk you thought it was real. You were very still, and the light from the moon and streetlamp was perfect, so I painted you. You couldn't see me. I could hear your music. I like Mahler. If I had the money I would send off and buy some of his records. There's a place you can mail to for classical records."

I tried to speak again, holding my head. "Don't," she said. "You fell. I looked up and you were gone. I was worried. I found you in the cave. Your blood was turning to ice. I brought you in here and Naima helped me get you to bed. We've been up with you."

"I have to catch my bus, I have to go back."

"It's already run."

"What!"

You'll have to stay here a few days, until you're well."

"Where are my clothes?"

"Drying. You know, you said some pretty strange things."

"What do you mean?"

"Well, it's on tape."

"Do you know who I am, what I am?"

"A sot with a busted head," she said, rocking the child in her arms.

"What did I say?"

"Nothing really. You sounded as if you were praying. Really, you didn't say much. Nothing you and I can't forget."

The Priest's Tape

10.

BEN FALLOW'S TALE

Ben Fallow's Tale

When it finally fell time for my retirement – this was a few years ago, my late wife and I thought it would be best if we travelled *this* land, not Europe and South America – we'd seen enough of that, and in this way spending time, our time, in the places our favorite authors spent theirs; we wanted to really see and listen to the people they wrote about. I would like to point out, however, that we had originally planned to spend our last years in Africa, but my wife's illness prevented such a journey. Perhaps I will go there yet. Our friends thought we were crazy; they warned me about Annette; they said we were leaving too much unfinished work behind, especially our jobs. In my profession, after one retires, he is still eligible for any number of chairs or lectures at prestigious universities, here and abroad, and so we both counted on returning, eventually, to our work. I must confess that my wife was far more interested in her work – and others in hers, than is the case with me. It follows, naturally, that she and her work are much more popular than mine – especially at present, since the years after her death. She was known, among biographers in her trade which she said was more lonely than the sea, as the marvelous liar who finally turned to truth. I suppose this was due to her natural inclination towards making a myth out of the lives of authors throughout her books, then turning towards analysis in the final chapter – always a long chapter – to redeem herself. Just as all the dead poets moved their boats through dark and dawn and dreams, so did my wife take her chances in dealing with literature, reality, and myth. Her work grew around her on the warm, damp nights like a melon vine crawling over mulch. She seemed to turn most everything under. She was like a protoplasmic mirror who simply reflected back the work to itself, the work to its author—sometimes as if she were the author. Though I loved her, I thought her work of little consequence, like anyone of us looking back at the stars on a clear night. I often wonder why friends never confided this to me. I know I always gave them the chance to consider my work. Pater has said that all artistic endeavors drift towards music, which is the only art that has form as its subject matter. I have often tried to apply this to my wife's past.

The Morning Watch, a little book by Agee, she'd always considered a classic in need of a romantic critic. I pointed out to her that we should be thinking about planning our vacation, but I could not hesitate from adding, "Since the Romantics were Classicists and the Greeks truly Romantics, I think you need to re-appraise the *true* worth of your pursuits." And with that I turned off the light. She suggested we both would have plenty of time to sleep on it during our travelling.

We bought a new pick-up with a fourwheel drive, had a camper mounted on the bed, and a hitch was welded on the bumper for our run-about. We almost forgot about the trailer hitch, and I was lucky to find someone to do it so late at night so we could leave the next morning. The welders listed in the phone book wouldn't do it; finally, I got one of them to suggest an old man who might do it. He was retired and had insomnia he told me over the phone in a Russian accent, but he would do it. He was quick to point out that the younger men in the trade weren't any good anyway. I wasn't used to other people *telling* me what to do, but when I knelt down beside him, he told me to look away or what I'd see would damage my eyes. He hummed some Russian folks song as he worked, the rods glowing purple in his dark garage. I walked out in his side yard and said goodbye to the city; he looked almost unreal. I told him about our trip. "You go to Kansas, you go to Olmitz — I got brother there. Big man, got wheat farm and lot of books." I liked the way he pronounced "books." "You like talking with him. Drive tractor all day, drink case of beer, listen to waltzes on stereo in his cab. Got air-conditioned tractor. You go to Kansas have good time."

Our itinerary and the red lines on our map was a piece of scholarship in itself, a bit of literary cartography. I should point out that this list of journeys, some actually taken and others only proposed, was not prompted or subsidized by a publisher. And we had nothing in mind. We were out to see it all, not take notes on it. Our minds were *open*. However, we didn't see it all. We saw only a little of it. We'd been to the East coast, then through the Midwest, the Northwest, the West coast, the Southwest and Plains, but we had saved the entire South, that *monstrorum artifex* for last. I must admit that this is my description of the South, and I have always derived a secret pleasure from the fact that my wife never knew if I intended my phrase to mean a holy vessel of art or land full of monstrosities. After a brief passage through the land of Twain my wife persuaded me to drive towards Memphis, and from there on to Knoxville and Agee's country. We would save the deep South for last. And it was in the hills of Tennessee, camped on the bank of a creek and drinking illegal whiskey, that I finally took my wife to task about her work. I accused her of a nearly septuagenarian epicurism in her approach. I said I thought she was more interested in weak-minded men than in great literature. I told her she had failed at her job, which was one of commenting on the infinite census of ideas, and not one where she could go into the door of an author's imagination and drink with his life and listen to his lies. Like Stevenson in "A Chapter On Dreams," you are haunted by the brown color of your own imagination and not the shade of what is written, I told her. I said, on the other hand, that my life was one of pure literary criticism, that I had long since given up all poetic notions as to my talent, and that life lasts as long as the idea of the metaphor does; images mean nothing; the color of a man's pants or his speech patterns mean nothing. She slept well, I thought, during that night, for I did not know she was sleeping and only the light flies around our lantern were listening to what I was saying.

She died during the night in her sleeping bag. It was a down pallet which could have withstood temperatures well below zero. I just looked at her. The first thing I did was something I had never done the entire time of our marriage; I looked through *her* papers. I didn't really read them; just looking at them, feeling them was enough.

We were camped on a creek bank and to get back to the truck we had to go by way of the creek to the main body of water and then a landing. I put her in the boat and we started back. There was still fog on the water. The whole ride I don't even think I thought of her—as dead; when I got to the landing, I *remembered*. It was several miles in to the nearest phone. For some reason, I couldn't place a local call, but I did get through to friends and our family in the East. They made arrangements and said they would book me a flight. I kept trying the local circuits but couldn't get through. I noticed a man admiring my boat. When I told him my wife was dead he didn't seem shocked, even though she was still lying in the boat in the sleeping bag; rather, he had the expression: *Let me think about it awhile*. But he was most kind, directing me to the funeral home. In fact, he walked with me afoot. I had somehow gotten the truck and trailer in a position where I couldn't back up to turn around. In New York I thought back to this walk I took, I thought back often, comparing the ways we cared for the dead: our procedures were so unlike the gentle customs of that small town mortuary where I purchased her casket. I interrupted the undertaker's breakfast. He was quite a young man. At first I thought he was a servant, and the old black man in the blue suit seated with him at the table in the kitchen was the mortician. It was the young man who got up and came to the kitchen door, answering the knock of the man I was with, evidently a friend, while the other stayed seated, scraping the crust off his black toast. I thought it was odd that they invited me to breakfast. The parlor we later retired to smelled of smoked ham and coffee. While the young man and I spoke there, the man who brought me ate a bite with his helper. Of course, he didn't have any idea who I was, but he did understand my needs.

It wasn't the best, but it was next to best: a mahogany coffin with brass handles made by his father. It was just right. The best that he had, which looked more like an antique soldier's footlocker, was reserved for the honorable senator from their town. So this was where the Gray Ghost roamed, I thought, remembering our meeting at an anti-war rally. Gore from Tennessee. He and Fulbright from Arkansas gave rousing speeches. I asked the young man if I might visit the retired senator, and he told me that he would probably be reading the morning paper on his front porch this time of day. Things were done quickly. We took my wife's body into the front room of the old house and the black man said, "Let us have her now. I will prepare the body myself. We'll make ready for her journey to your home." He closed his eyes after every sentence.

I did walk by Senator Gore's house. He had on a plaid shirt to keep out the brisk morning. There were still flowers in his well-kept beds. He was asleep in the porch swing, and yesterday's *Times* was blowing across his front lawn. I did not wake him.

I was very hungry and stopped in at a fisherman's cafe. Most of the fishermen were gone, of course. I thought how it would be eating without my wife. Whenever she was gone, I ate compulsively; she was always getting me trimmed down on her diets. I could see myself five years from then. I ordered eggs; eggs only, and beer. I ate thirteen fried eggs with running yellows. There were spots of blood in each yolk. These were country eggs. The beer didn't go well with them, but I kept drinking it.

Some said I should stay at home: they tried to persuade me to go back to teaching, accept various posts, get started on other books. None thought it wise for me to return, to pick up on the travels alone, the travels she had booked for us, but I was determined now more than ever to spend time in those places. One night in Memphis and only a few days in Tennessee. No, those hours in the Gray Ghost's home town convinced me. She'd worked years on the map in secret—I'd found several, tattered maps she'd worked with, but it was more out of lack of interest, and not respect, that I didn't dip further into her papers. I found one interesting item concerning our trip, an unaddressed post card, the note unfinished: "We'll *both* die in the South if we try to cover all its ground, so we are forced to limit outselves to one author, one genre for each state—no more."

I looked on her desk at the photographs, the many photographs of her and her family gallivanting on their grounds and around their large, white hosue. She was proud of her past, her reputation—both her reputations, family and literary biographer; she still hadn't changed. As we had visited her home state many times, and since it was not endowed with *anyone* of any literary stature whatsoever, I assure you, and it was the only such state in the South, I took it for granted that there would not be a red pencil line past her old home. I was wrong. I did find such directions, and on the new map we were using, a blue line made with a heavy hand, parallelling the river, and ending with an X miles from any other hamlet or maintained road. I'd noticed such a routing that day in the hills of Tennessee, but I thought it nothing more than a doodle. But *there* was an X. Did she consider herself worthy of the company of the authors: No, she didn't. Besides, her place of birth was far from the X.

As soon as I was out of the foothills of Tennessee and travelling on flatter ground, I tried to stay on dirt, gravel, and along water as much as possible. It was a bit of a temptation not to stopover in Memphis, having had only one night there before; I did want to see my old friend, but if I were really to abide by the rules of her list the fact that he was still living disqualified him. So I crossed the big river and took the worst roads I could, the ones that followed the levees and the roads that were on the levees themselves.

I drove past her family's old home without stopping just as one drives past the residences of those he has had a falling out with, but the fact is I'd never had a falling in with them, only with their daughter, and that was many, many years ago.

My left arm was much redder than my right. The air-conditioner had stopped working in Kentucky but I'd not stopped anywhere to have it repaired. And I was leery of shade-tree mechanics, although if I could have found someone as trustworthy as the old Russian I would not have hesitated. I was getting near the end of her directions. There seemed to be a few travellers leaving *there* that warm morning, a boy on a mule with a pole, a gypsy family in a wagon with a huge palm painted on either side, a man on a tractor in a suit coat over his overalls, and a pretty young girl in a yellow dress on a bicycle, but none of them were going *there*. I seemed to be the only one heading that way. Here were the people I'd seen and heard only in the imaginations of other men and women. I drove very slowly, in the lowest gear, just poking along, trying to *imagine* myself driving along the levee. I could not. And then, in the mirror, I noticed the girl in the yellow dress following me, eating my dust. I stopped, she passed by, eating a lime, holding the handle bars with one hand, and only glancing my way. All of a sudden she turned down the slope of the levee and coasted at a terrific speed down to a field where she disappeared.

Not far from the sign MANTENANCE ENDS HERE – which was misspelled, I could see the holes in the road before I felt them. Some state or county workers were sitting in the shade of their truck, drinking ice water and eating cup cakes and laughing. The water looked good, and I thought I could kill both birds if I asked some directions. I could see they admired my camper and boat, then they looked at my shoes and watch and hair.

"Saw your water and it looked good," I said, deepening my voice, and speaking to all of them.

"Hep yourself."

"Mighty hot."

"It'll get worst."

"I guess you four live around here?"

"Yea," one of them was doing all the talking.

"Anyplace up here to camp?"

"Camp! Unless you're figuring on collecting a bill I wouldn't stay down that road long."

"Why?"

"Why! Those niggers gone and lected them a black-assed Congresswoman. They settling in there like bees on honeysuckle. Lest you some kind of troublemaker – you ain't are you – I don't see why you'd want to *camp* there. You, boys?"

"Nah."

"Hell no, I'd stay out a there Mister."

These were the kind of men I'd read about, the kind I hated. I hated them because I didn't understand them. And because I didn't understand them, I feared them. But I knew I could go there, I could go anywhere I wanted. It was they who would be in danger if they went there, not I.

"Yea," one of them said, "I hear they got a surveyor hired to go in there and get all the land straightened out once and for all and everybody white that's got land in there is gone get rid of it. Ain't no count noway. Heard that up at the courthouse. Aw hell, you can look around if you want to, but I damn sure wouldn't spend one night there. If you wanting to camp, there's a Govment ground back up the road and off to the right about forty mile. Hell fire, them Bentwell niggers carry round rifles in their pick-ups. They getting that Govment money now, see. Got stereo tapes in their trucks. One of um got a airplane. No lie. Well, there's white people in there alright, but they old and strange. They's white people that live there but I sho don't know what for. Ya'll boys?"

"Nah," they all hummed, looking down at the ground.

"No, Mister, they went and lected um a nigger, and there's no telling what is gone happen. . . ."

"Well, I thank you for the water," I said, cutting him off.

As I drove away, he called out, "They'll steal that boat!"

I saw shacks near the fields, shacks over the water, one large and run-down mansion, a store and a drinking joint, a fix-all, a church with the steeple blown over and on the ground, a man walking the other way towards a stalled car I'd passed and carrying a battery, many people working and others asleep on porches, a seed and feed, a schoolhouse with men working on the roof, but I saw more than that.

They sold gas at the store. I honked, and a stout, red-faced woman walked down the steps carefully and slowly, and pumped my gas without saying a word. I had no idea on earth where I was. The surroundings didn't seem to correspond with the map. Intending to say something more than, "Hot," which was all I could get out before she interrupted me with, "Aint it," something suddenly occurred to me, and this was that the blue line and X may have meant no more than a place where we could launch our boat; afterall, these maps you pick up at the service stations are known to be off. I knew I was where she had planned us to be but, by the map, the water should have been eight miles to the west. I could see the water. I asked the lady if she knew of a place I might camp for the day and night. I told her I was just a sightseer. She told me a spot further down the road. She noticed my out of state tags and I saw her nod to herself, as if she self-affirmed her own suspicions. I could see curiosity grow on her fat face like a tomato on a vine. She seemed a kind woman, though; the kind that would bend over backwards to please you. As I paid her, I asked with a smile, "Say, do you know of any famous people who have come from around here?"

She smelled the five dollar bill and broke out with a huge laugh, "Not hardly!" Her belly shook like a bucket of water.

I camped close enough to the river to hear the fish jumping at night, just as we had by the creek when Annette died. I lit the lantern and took out a new copy of the novella she'd worn out over the years, Agee's *The Morning Watch*. I suppose I did read a few chapters, but I really couldn't keep my mind on it. I was bothered by the fact that I couldn't concentrate on something my wife could immerse herself in. I was bothered by bugs; what was I doing there? Something was odd. Why on earth had she planned to come to this spot? I put down the book and got the map from her old copy of Agee's story, the magazine *Botteghe Oscure*. I went over the names of the surrounding towns and communities, trying to place them with some author, with some work. Was it possible that she had found out certain biographical data on someone was incorrect; perhaps she was working on some obscure allusion to the area; maybe some writer had a long, lost love in the territory; but she would have certainly told me. Before I bedded down, I dashed off some quick notes to those of her colleagues she trusted most, asking whether or not they could link any author to this place. I would mail them at the Post Office in the little store the next morning. I turned the light down, hoping the bugs would go, and spread repellent on, and opened the book once again. *The night smelled like new milk.* . . .

My night was bad. It was too warm to sleep well. Of course, at my age, I am accustomed to all sorts of dreams. Mostly, I always end up sharing the same fate as do certain literary beings, but this night of dreams was different. My wife was a young woman. She was tall, and thin again with auburn hair. She was sitting in an elegant chair near the edge of the water. In a very soft voice she was lecturing to a group of schoolboys. They were sitting at her feet, spellbound, dressed in wool blazers, shorts, long gray socks, and odd caps with some kind of sewn-in writing on them. All but one. He was naked. He was washing himself in the river. From time to time she looked at him to see if he were paying attention, but he was not. A dark hog kept grunting and rooting near her feet. Her feet were bare. The boy walked from the water to where she was seated. He unbraided her hair. She washed his genitals with her hair. He ran off with the hog. I saw him kneeling down, sucking milk from a cow. There was a dead calf beside the cow, and the hog was rooting through its brain. Annette told the boys to come back the next evening. They left. As soon as they could no longer see her, she unbuttoned her dress and lay her breast in her palm. A light rain began to fall. I could smell the rain in the dream.

Someone had visited me during the night. They'd taken my cooler full of iced-downed food and they had done something else. Someone had nailed a black water moccasin to a tree not twelve feet from where I slept. It had writhed itself to death during the night, leaving a trickle of blood on the bark, and now it was getting ripe and drawing flies. Big, dark flies that sounded like machines in a factory in the city.

It was the only night I was really in mourning for Annette. And the dream was too simple for a man in my shoes to spend the time explicating.

Her handwriting was ambiguous. Did her itinerary show this to be the last stop of our journey through the South, or did she mean it was really to be the final stop? Unless she was deceiving me, I knew she planned to travel through the other states. I knew she did. So why the last stop? Did she have some erroneous premonition as to the exact location where she would die? Was X marking the spot of her death? It *was* near her home, but there had to be something else. It was certainly conceivable she was about to share with me information heretofore unknown. Perhaps that was her sense of dramatic, letting me know something then. After all, she *was* who she was. The reputation of her family and her career was matched only by her imagination.

I handed over the letters to a kindly old maid behind the bars of the P.O. It seemed that she had a feud going with the big woman who kept the store, and I'd just stepped in the middle of it. I don't know if they were mother and daughter or what, but each was telling the other to keep U.S. Postal and store business separate. The old lady dabbed the stamps on her tongue several times. I was fascinated with their age; they were faded and dusty. They were so old, collectors items perhaps, that it took quite a few of them to suffice for the current rates. She was intrigued by my letters, especially their well out of state destinations. But when I told her she might as well send them all Special Delivery, she sighed like an old woman does, apologized for the fact that there wasn't anymore room on the front of the envelopes—but she'd see that they got there just the same, and immediately forgot the ongoing feud, by calling out, "Quick Faye, tell Luther we've got a bundle of Air Mail Specials; tell him to hurry!" "Luther's been the mailman here a awful long time, but things is getting slow now. The Govment sent us a little motor scooter to deliver mail on, but Luther don't ever use it. He lets those kids ride it. Land sakes, Luther's got his work cut out for him this afternoon. I hope he's not on one this week."

Why not pick a few groceries up while I was there, I thought. I didn't want the undertaking of leaving so soon. And by all means, I didn't want to start their fussing again. I was careful to ask the big woman in charge of the store, calling for light bread, milk, chips, beans, lunch meat, a carton of smokes, and beer.

"We don't sell alcohol here, you'll have to get that across the road, but I can fix you up with the rest. Hatti will fix your sandwiches for you if you want. Won't you Hatti? Put him a slice a cheese and some that new goose liver we got. He'll like that special. Mr. uh . . ., would you mind if I thowed in some lima beans? I got so many this year me and Hatti won't ever eat them, and nobody round here is going to buy them. Say, did you ever find that famous person you'se a looking for. Last night I did some special thinking. There was a famous person come from here, born right over there on that island."

"Yes, who? Who?" I wanted to know.

"Dudley Wells. Hatti's got a picture of him over there in the P.O. somewhere. He's on the G-Men's Ten Most Wanted List," she said, laughing.

I shared her laugh, but was a bit disappointed. I was on my way out, sack in my arms, when Hatti grabbed me by the arm.

"There used to be a correspondence here . . . long ago. You'd have to ask Luther. Correspondence with someone in the East . . . a woman. Yes, I believe it was. Luther'd know. She must have been colored, because it was a colored man who wrote her. What was his name. . . ."

To my knowledge, there has been no literary investigation and research to ever yield such stunning results as this, the facts of which I have only recently uncovered and documented. As a professional historian, I use the term *recently* accordingly. We have all suffered our enchantments with authors and their work — in any case, the ideas behind their work, those men and writing living and dead, profound and unfortunate, genius and talent, imaginary and real; but to be related — by blood, so to speak — to such a literary adventure, pregnant with intrigue and notorious figures, might well prove to be far more than I can endure, more than I can understand. I can forgive men's ideas and sometimes their actions, but not their imaginations. For more than not they lead to this, a *regressus in infinitum*. My wife had bequeathed me such a nexus of art and reality, a dizzying, reducing mirror of her past, more unfocused than the poet's mind. And it was her favorite, Mallarmé, who said we exist so we can be written in a book. Another life lost in images, another succedaneum for a work of art. On the one hand, I was anxious to learn everything, to drill into the hollowness of her ideas, her spontaneous life; while on the other hand, I must admit, I was afraid to confront the dream of *ars combinatoria*, I was afraid the lasting inventions of the mind would be superseded by the technology of the imaginative life. And when one is seventy years old this is a fear akin to oblivion, a doubting which leads to a confrontation between essence and appearance once again, a fear which makes one afraid to choose what to love, one or the other, faith or theology, art or artists. An old man does not like and is not prepared to erase his tapes of Bach on the spot so he can listen to a drunk mailman expose his dead wife's secret past.

And so, without letting old Hatti know who I was or what I was up to, I made certain the person she spoke of was Annette. Next, I had her arrange a meeting with Luther. They told me he drank, so I got liquor from across the street to loosen his tongue from the black Socratic stance I knew he would take. And I did erase great music, so I could record whatever he said.

The evening was made with whippoorwills and mosquitos. After the moon rose, the insects seemed to flow like those dark molecules of blood floating in our eyes. Luther showed up on time, riding a white jackass. I suppose you could call the man a black Fields if you needed some sort of recognizable touchstone of personality. He wanted you to know he knew that he knew that you knew that he knew he was pretending. He acted like he knew nothing, when in fact he knew a great deal. And so he was like looking into several peer glasses that kept reflecting and diminishing his image. His words were at once simple and complex. And he liked to drink and wander through the thickets of his past.

"Said a man wanted Luther," I heard him say as he rode up, still dressed in postman's clothes, safari hat and all.

"Yes! You don't know me. This might take awhile. Do you think you'd have the time to get down and drink with a stranger?"

"Think I will, think I will."

"Hot as hell isn't it?"

"What you want with me, Mister?"

"Fallow . . . Ben Fallow's the name."

"Pleased. My name is Luther Coover."

"How long have you been working at the P.O.?" I asked him, taking a cork out of a bottle.

"Miss Eleanor Roosevelt got me my job. A many year ago and I'm proud to say it."

"Been there awhile have you?"

"Awhile."

"How about something to drink?"

"Yea, I'll take some, but look. I didn't come over here to beat round no bush. What's on your mind. I'll drink your liquor all night with you, but let me know where I stand right now. Luther Coover not no fool. . . ."

"So you don't have to try to fool me, here," I said, handing him a drink.

"Thanks. I hope you got a whole lot of that."

"Do you remember many of the people who gave you letters?"

"Good, you coming right to it. Yes, some of them."

"Would you happen to remember delivering letters with a handwriting like this?" I asked, giving him an envelope.

He held the piece of paper up to the moon. "This here's a woman's handwriting on this."

"I know. So what do you say?"

"I don't know if I'm saying anything yet."

"There won't be any trouble . . . none. I can give you my word. The woman who had this handwriting is dead." I told him, without letting on she was my wife. But I knew he suspected something, and I know he knew *that*.

"Well, then Mister Ben Fallow, all three of them is dead, and that sho makes a difference. I suspect it makes a heap of difference."

"What do you mean?"

"I mean her son's dead, and his father's been dead a long time; now, she's gone. Don't time fly?"

II

I am one of those who believe that every word has been permeated just as every image has been transmuted, through the mindful intensity and control of one constraining act, and it overwhelms the weary imagination when it finds it has overlooked those acts. For example, from the story by Bierce:

A Woman in widow's weeds was weeping upon a grave.

"Console yourself, madam," said a Sympathetic Stranger.

"Heaven's mercies are infinite. There is another man somewhere, besides your husband, with whom you can still be happy."

"There was," she sobbed—*"There was, but this is his grave."*

And so it is with this widower: he must admit he was wrong about the logical connection of his wife and himself, nothing followed from their mutual pasts, only something else was created, something fascinating and at the same time painful. I am reminded of the scene in the film by Cocteau where the fragments and shards of the broken mirror flow mysteriously back into themselves to form another mirror, another image.

Luther only told me a little that night; he could see he was hurting me, and so he would wander off in other directions only to come back to Annette and the other two, reminding me why I had really asked him to come to my camp by the river. We both drank too much. We ran out of whiskey, turned to what beer I had in the cooler, then hit bottles of wine I had picked up along the way, ones I'd planned to age and drink in ten years. He did not like me calling him Luther and he did not like me calling him Mr. Coover; he would grimace at me as if I were a bad smell. I settled for Coover and he called me old man — although he was older than I, or Ben Fallow as if it were one, Jewish name. The white jackass of his would neigh at the moon like it was a palm full of sugar, and Coover would pick up an empty can or bottle and hit the beast in the head.

"Let it rest, Ben Fallow. Let the bygones be gone. Nothing to explain. The past you can't never explain; nothing adds up. It's like the river I tell you, you ain't never looking at the same thing, it keeps on running, changing, moving, it ain't no use to try to follow it. Look here. Look at what you got there. Nice speedboat and a truck, and I bet you got a big empty house up where you live, full of nice things, nice memories, and you bound to have family of your own, chilluns and chillun of chillun by now, you not hurting white man, you got all you need. I wished I was in your shoes — how about loaning me five? What we need. . . ."

"... Is something more to drink!"

"Now you talking that field talk, Ben Fallow."

"Where do we get it this time of morning?"

"Don't you worry, I know a place don't ever shut down because it don't ever open up. But listen here, ain't nobody but me finding out who you are around here. Ya'll could of helped that boy. But we going. You got to know the password to get in this place, and Luther Coover knows it."

Like a vivid dream you can't remember the details of, I was confounded by the sharp and jagged edges of the life that Coover was putting together. Many times, during the long conversations with him, I let my mind drift also into the pasts of men passing on tales around fires in ancient fields and ancient halls. At times I came to the conclusion that Coover talked to no one but himself, that he entertained listeners who were ghosts. He always seemed to be aware of a stage, and beleaguered by the fact there was no audience, yet he kept on performing, making these little wisecrack asides out of his own misery and the woes of others. A sadder and kinder man I had never known.

"Hey Ben Fallow. You know what they used to call me in the old days, back in the old days when I was in show business; they called me The Whistling Nigger. You want to hear me whistle some?"

"No. I want you to tell me how to drive to this place, this joint we're going to, so we can get something to drink."

"Don't you mind about that. We'll get there alright. Only thing you mind about is this, don't you let anybody know who you are. Don't you let Miss Hatti know up there at the store, and don't you let her daughter know, and especially don't you let on out here where we're going. You get drunk, you watch your tongue."

"Why?"

"Why! That woman could of took care of that boy better than she did."

"Look Coover, you're talking about my wife. She did alot of

good, she wrote lots of books. She was a old woman when she died. I know I would have done things different, had I known. I would have seen to things."

"Yea, ya'll are all time seeing to things alright, seeing to this, seeing to that."

My eyes and my mind were whirring like the frogs in the trees. Little by little, Coover was filling in the dark reflection of Annette's past, but I hadn't the heart to stop him, ask him to explain. It was like an opera; I had to listen to the whole thing. He gave me all the right directions to the dive, where to turn and when to turn out my headlights. We both wanted to talk about other things – two men wanted to drink and carry-on together, we wanted to forget, but Annette was ever in my mind and the boy in his. He asked me if I had a knife. I said yes, there was one in my tackle box. He asked me if I had money to lend. I said yes. He told me around here the folks wouldn't understand if they knew who I was. They liked the boy, and they didn't think my wife did right by him.

Just as we were approaching the place I ran the truck off into a ditch. We weren't thirty yards from the joint. Everyone seemed to be fairly worn out, sitting at their tables trying to stay awake. One man with no shirt, who was probably on something, Coover said, was playing the conga drums. A black and white T.V. set was playing away also, but with no sound and no viewers. We got out of the truck, and managed to stagger over to the front steps of the shack. They barely lifted their heads, not seeming to care, until they saw me. Coover said in the whole time the place had been there no man or woman had ever told the law the password; he said that unknown people, black and white, had to say the passwords even if they were with regular customers. So, in a French not at all like this, Coover whispered in my ear: *Mille astres de la nuit n'eclairent pas un seul lit*, and I said the same.

"The boy put them words on us a long time ago. He was fine with words. Walked up one evening, now that was when Spann's wife was living—she had French blood in her, and Spann say, "Evening, Dunbar." And Dunbar say, well, he say those pretty words. Spann say, "Come again." So Dunbar, he said them again. This time Spann's wife heard them. She said, "I say, Spann, with these words nobody from town going to come no way." And so that night Dunbar got drunk and said words like that all night till day, and got everybody to say them right. Miss that boy."

"What was his name?"

"Yes. Dunbar. Dunbar Lewis."

We sat down and ordered, leaning over the table and speaking low. There was a ceiling fan turning and before Coover's story was over the blades of the fan were cutting me with their shadows. It would be daylight, but before that there was still hours of darkness.

"You ever hear that name around your place? You ever see it around? I don't guess you did. You ever read about him. Didn't your wife say anything bout him when he went to jail. I don't guess nobody ever heard of him till after he died. I hate to think about those last few years."

"No, I never did. I don't know him from the moon. That is the reason I'm staying here. I know now why my wife wanted to come. What about his father?"

"Shoot. We got plenty of time to talk about him. He wasn't much."

"Coover," I said, putting my hand on his shoulder, "I know you don't think much of me, or my wife, but I want you to tell me everything."

"Keep your voice down."

"You don't have to tell it from then to now, just start anywhere, help me construct his life."

It is quite serious to live around another's flaws, especially when you are married to them. Still again, it is a tragedy for you to find these flaws to be deep faults after this loved one is dead. I could, with object distance, understand and forgive for her trying to protect the reputation of her family, but I saw something more than that. I was sure there was something more. And later I was to find this hunch of mind to be true. I saw her trying to cover over her past for professional reasons, but I did not understand her reasoning. Sure, several Southern universities had backed her in the past, but it would be far from them to change their minds about her work — when her past was mirrored. God knows, the places I've worked for in the East would welcome such an adventure, simply to break the dullness. It gave me this sick feeling — I think it was the source, Coover did not; like a hand trying to put a nut on a bolt in my guts, some kind of turning and screwing in my belly.

"You see them flowers out there in the light, under the blue light pole. Those crawling blossoms. Spann been trying to cut them out of there for years. Dunbar told him he couldn't ever get rid of it. Dunbar called it wisteria. Spann just call it creeper, he say it choking all his fruit trees out. You see it strangling anything out there?"

"It's too dark out there for me to see."

"You sho got a cat eating your liver, don't you?"

I nodded my head. "What about correspondence, didn't she ever write the father?"

"Well, I can't rightly say. Let me think awhile. Can't remember if she sent Dunbar's old man money or not. I remember those letters that came. He wrote her a lot for awhile. Wrote her long letters. I thought that was all they were at first. But every month there came a check, not a big check now, but something every month. And I don't believe there was a letter in there. He knew she knew. He knew she was white and she knew he was a nigger, he was black. I don't know if there was an earlier letter or not. Something saying not to ever meet. Never seen one another. Never sent a picture. It was strange, something there I just couldn't understand. Then I couldn't, and I still can't, even with what I know now. It was as if — oh I don't know how to splain it."

"Did he have any education?"

"What you mean! Did he have any education? That boy was smart. Smart man, knew more than anybody round here. He had a head on his shoulders. And it all didn't come from his mother, either. He done part of it hisself, but that nocount daddy of his knew lots himself. He had had a job as a tutor in somebody's home in Africa somewhere. Then he done something like that aboard ship for people travelling somewhere, but nobody liked him. He really wasn't round here long, just came and goed as he liked, never staying long, always out of money and luck. But he wasn't a blockhead, not by a long shot. His mind was always occupied. He knew shit from shinola, let's put it that way."

There was a boy stealing a boiled egg out of a large jar on the counter. No one but me saw him, and he saw me looking at him. He put his finger to his lips, and slipped back down in front of the counter, out of view, looking at the Tarzan picture on the screen. I don't know if he had the sound turned down so only he could hear it, or what. Tarzan was swimming through an enemy river with a knife in his mouth, and natives were throwing spears at him.

"He went off to college, he was passing see, he went off to college, and I don't know, I don't think she sent him too much money to go to college on, I don't know, I got to let it all come back, I been trying to forget it all so long, maybe she did send him some, but he got one them scholarships, you'll have to look at your check stubs. But he grew up with some women lived over there on the other side of the river, what they called that bend over there I can't place, I can't remember. That's where they lived. Now maybe your wife wrote them. Maybe that's who. Goddamn man, it's been so long ago, leastways it seems that way. They would of got their mail different, but I know he got his mail right there. He went to school, and started hanging round white girls I guess. I believe there was one in particular. I don't know what her name was. Yea I do. Things are cloudy, but I'm recollecting. Hung around with a white girl. So you really want to know about him? Maybe after I tell you about him you won't want to know, you'll be sorry you know, you'll be sorry you came down here and started messing around. But if you have to, I'll tell you. Mind now, I'm not saying everything I say is true, or the way it really happened; I'm not saying I saw all or heard all, but this is what folks have told me and this is what I do know. This is what he told me, too. He grew up with some women on the island over there. I guess he was like all the boys, he played over there all the time, except he just kept to himself. I think it was a mistake he found out; he got into one of the letters from your wife to one of the Sister women taking care of him. Now, he found out through hook or crook someway, somehow, don't ask me. Got into one of those letters. Then he hitchhiked to Memphis, got him a library card, started looking up all those books your wife had written, those books on the great people. I never read one of them, but he had them all. He worked day and night so he could buy them; he just didn't like the library owning them. Right then and there is when he decided he was gone be like them. Guess that was the worst thing to get into him; started on him like a earworm in sweetcorn. He told me a story one time. The first few years he lived by himself. He didn't start off living with black people, somehow he got in the hands of an old white man. All that came later. He was just out of the womb when the white fisherman got him. I'll tell you. He was some old nocount, some old trash who lived on the river. They called him trash, I never knowed him to be trash, I never seen him that much. He was an old river rat hermit what he was. The boy was living with him. One day they was out fishing, one winter day. He'd been sick for a long time. The man couldn't even row his boat. They was out there together, making what living they could. They was using some bird liver or something on the trot line going down. It was a real cold morning, out there in the boat. They'd been fishing and the old man said, 'Son, let me lay my head in your lap.' Son-of-a-bitch. Spann, we come here to drink, not to dream. You paying ain't you? The boy wrapped him up in blankets and let him lay his head down. Man said, 'Boy, I got to tell you something.' 'What you got to say, Pop,' the boy said. 'I got to tell you that I ain't your Pop.' I guess the boy was about four or five year old then. 'You ain't my Pop, then who is?' he say. 'I don't know. Don't know who he is, but they ain't nobody else round here going to take you but me. Don't guess no white folks want you. I know your mother is living, but I don't know nothing else about her. Listen, it's best you just live a good life, and remember me, remember that I loved you.' The old man's throat was filling up with blood, he couldn't hardly talk, he was coughing, and that old stuff was down in his lungs, he had what the Sister women called the death rattling. He say, 'Son, I hate to tell you this, but you part nigger; you can take that fillet knife and cut my throat for telling you.' The old man died, and the boy rowed him back to the shore. He picked him up, I just don't know. I don't know how a four year old boy could drag a dead man up the bank like that, dig a hole, and bury him, but he did. It must have took him all night. Maybe two days. But he sure enough did. I guess he lived there by hisself awhile. Nobody knowed about it. One day two big old fat women were down there, bank fishing. Black women, a colored women. Uh, I'm going to get it yet. And they saw that boy, and he ran off when they seen him. They knew that old hermit lived there with some kid, so they thought they better go check in on it. They found the boy had shut himself up in the outhouse, and he was reading aloud out of the Bible, found the old man's grave, and a nice looking garden. Somebody had come to seen him through in those years, cause the boy was reading books. They was a stack of them in the shack. And for sure that old hermit didn't teach him. What they suspected was that the old critter sent a letter someway off to the boy's daddy — somebody had to wrote it, telling him he didn't have long for this world, and he better come see about his son. His daddy come there awhile, but the sea got in his blood again, or those drums, and he lit out, leaving the boy high and dry and by hisself. Least, he taught him how to read and write while he was there. The boy probably lived there alone from then on until those big women got hold on him. He never did go to the colored school, never did go to the white school, just learned on his own. Maybe one those women knew a preacher or somebody who could help him. He learned all the subjects he should, got books somewhere, all except he didn't have the boyfriends and girlfriends like he should. Didn't have no companionship his own age. Them old women died on him, left him just enough to get through until he became of age. Right then he left, went off somewhere on a boat. Some say he thought about going East, but I believe he stayed down here, somewhere around where there was Greeks, like around New Orleans. Fishing was all he knew how to do, but he really knew plenty. They was having plenty of those ships to go down then, and one of those Greeks taught him hard hat salvage diving. Dangerous work, but you make plenty. He didn't stay with it long, came on back here, started drinking heavy. With all the money he had on him for awhile, there was some who say he turned crooked. That was a lie, that boy was about as crooked as a lightpole. What he did was this: he rowed a boat over there to that college town, found a big, beat-up old house up on top of a mountain at the edge of town. He had enough money to pay the rent for a few months. I think it used to be a whorehouse, I ain't sure anymore. Lived there alone on top of the mountain, and got into the rabbit raising business somehow, just long enough to earn what he need to buy books and enroll in that college. He must of put one over on them bout his high school. He took everything he could afford, everything they'd let him. And I mean he flat told them; he put some grades on them they still haven't forgot. Well, they gave him a scholarship, of course. And a lot of the men took a interest in him; they went out their way helping him out, loaning him money for clothes and books and rent and things. There was one old great big professor who was even paying his liquor bill. Give him money to go to the show. I'm not saying whether or not they knew he wasn't white. But they knew he had a head on his shoulders. Then a girl come along and fell in love with him, stayed up in that house on the hill with him. The boy started drinking, see. Them professors knew he was cut out for something. I wished I was with him on those women, though. He didn't know nothing about them. Either she done him bad, or he done her wrong; what's the difference. Me and you know, we's old enough to know, we found out how love is, clouds at night, moving while you're sleeping, a big dark field where hogs have been. See, he never was with them when he was coming up, cept those big ladies. Should of been growing up with them. Didn't know nothing about them; I guess he was a little bit fraid of them. And he was so good looking and he didn't know what to do with himself with women, well now, naturally, I say naturally, them other kinds started trying to mess with them. He never did let them. But there was one of them, I'll say it, he was a queer, you know, and he was a good queer, you know, because he understood the boy's situation, I guess he wasn't out for his own self, he was out to become the boy's daddy, I guess you could say he loved him like that — which ain't wrong at all. The queer understood the boy didn't really want him to mess with him, he just needed talking, he knew he didn't have no folks and was messed up about women; see, what happened was this, when the boy was a young one a bunch of white girls came out to the river and found him, I don't know what they did to him, whether they got him drunk or give him loco weed, but they really messed him up. They got him down on the ground and done something to him. The man really took him in, he was a little man named Henry, Henry Cross, he was a real smart man just like Dunbar, so they got along like two peas in a pod, I think he taught Greek and things like that, he was the one who took him in after the boy started messing up. Nobody else would have anything to do with him, cause he started drinking and not going to his classes, not reading what they told him. The rest of them just said to hell with him, but he helped him out, fed him, got him books, helped him pay his rent. The man, Henry, told him, 'Son, I believe you're some kind of artist.' Told him he ought to take courses in art, and dancing, and writing, stuff like that. Said he saw something in him, said he ought to try to bring it on out of himself. Said there was some kind of buried, fallen star deep down in him, something burned, and he ought to dig it out with a sharp knife. Least, that's what Dunbar told me he said. Well, as it turned out, it seems like every time this boy gets tied in with somebody that really wanted him to do good, do right by him, they die on him. And that's what happened. The boy went home one day and found Henry dead as hell, talking, I mean listening to his own voice on one of them big taping machines, like Spann got over there to record songs he likes on the radio. See, he'd been translating on something, I'll recollect the name of it in a minute, and he died listening to himself. The provision in the will said the boy was to be taken care of the rest of his life, but somehow they twisted it around where the boy didn't get nothing but a few books and records. Not one red cent. Dunbar still had that big place up on top of the mountain, so he pulled out of school, took what he had back up there, lived by himself. Well, Henry had told somebody at the college about Dunbar, some music professor called Goll. The man sent Dunbar a note, saying he'd like him to enroll as a music student. You got to imagine now, Ben Fallow, cause that Dunbar couldn't even play spoons. He couldn't play a lick of music, not one lick on nothing. He couldn't even beat a drum. I seen him once, when he was little, pick up a guitar. He put it under his arms, leaned his head down over it, strummed it, and a string broke, I'm not lying, it broke and a black widow spider crawled out of that hollow place. That son-of-a-bitch couldn't blow a tune on a pop bottle. But he could whistle, yes he could, but that was only on account of me. Well, Dunbar took that letter up to the Music Department. They asked him to play what he could. So he whistled some blues by Robert Johnson and Forest City Joe Pugh and John Lee Hooker, and some things like "Greensleeves," told them that was about all he could do. I guess it was about his twentieth year, I don't remember. Course, that Goll couldn't waste his time on him, but they shoved him into one of these beginning classes where you listen. And right here is where it all starts. The teacher is a woman. She's older than him, very beautiful. She's married and has children of her own. She plays the piano and the cello and God knows what all. Dunbar told me. What he said, she was like a port of shadows — dig that, it's the kid talking, your wife's boy, he can't play no violin, but he can talk a mean line — and he was an empty barge. You hear that Ben Fallow, I say wake up. Your boy talking."

"Not mine," I told him.

"Lord, he came up with some lines, Dunbar did. Fell in love soon as he stepped into the room. She knew there was something about him she liked, but she didn't know what it was."

"I know what it was."

"Ben Fallow, I feel sorry for you. You don't know your ass from a hole in the ground and you seventy years old. White man, my heart goes out to you, like a decoy floating near you blind. You don't know shit, Ben Fallow. You still hung up. You know I don't know whether to believe you or not. Sometimes I think you don't really care, you not down here to find out what you say. You still got something in your craw. With you, I really think it comes down to this: your wife screwed a nigger, had a nigger baby . . . boy child that weren't yours. Am I right?"

"Part of the time . . . it's something old in the heart, gone bad, something that smells, that stinks to high heaven, a rotten seeping wound even a man like me, a man who thinks he knows, has to lick."

"Forget it Ben Fallow, I'm telling you. You know, I think I like you. You're telling me the truth, you ain't feeding me shit. Ben Fallow ain't so dumb after all I say. Lord, I'm glad I ain't white, ain't got all those sins to keep begging mercy for. Hell, Ben Fallow, you done what you had to do, you stood up, you said what you said, I respect that, but I believe I like you more for what you just done. You admitted something, something true. I trust you. I'm going to help you find out what you want to know. Once, a long time ago, I was walking down a long, dusty road, and it was hot as hell, I was just a boy, I was carrying ice to my family. I look down the road, and Luther says to himself, look there, a great long black snake crawling up ahead, coming after Luther to sip the ice. But Ben Fallow, that weren't no snake, that was a mirage you see when the sunlight is bearing down. Now I'm telling you I was mighty afraid, I knowed it was a snake, I felt it, you know it's like a dream, it don't really happen and again it does, and that's how it is with your wife, and her son. You'd a been proud of him. Maybe you could of ended up writing bout him; but he probably wasn't your style, wasn't nothing . . ."

"Lightning outside. Is it going to rain?"

"All that is . . . is heat lightning. Won't rain here. Just light. You know it's mighty strange you ask me that. One night me and Dunbar was sitting in here, and it was making like that out in the night. And I ask him that, I asked then if — him and that woman — a rain was going to set in, if that lightning meant anything. You know what he said, he said in that story of Romeo and Juliet there was something like a *lightning before death*, he asked me whatever I reckoned he saw. Well, he was drunk, so I never payed no attention. I just wanted to know if my melons was going to grow, my White River Rattlesnakes, that's all I ever tried to grow. Need lots of sandy loam . . ."

"A *lightning before death*, wait, I think I remember hearing my wife say that over and over to herself. Yea, she used to say that sometimes, at her desk, sometimes in her sleep."

"Well, I told you they wrote for awhile. Bound to heard it from him. Hell, he wrote down whatever floated into his mind. I guess that's what the woman liked about him — whatever floated into his mind. She didn't know he wasn't all white, she didn't care, it wasn't that, it was something else fascinated her. See, she told everybody in the class to put on their headphones, then she played them pieces of music. She cut in with this machine on everybody's listening, one at a time, asking them what the music meant to them. She got down to Dunbar Lewis, she said his name over the line going into his ear, she say, 'Mr. Dunbar Lewis, your impression on this.' I don't guess she ever stopped listening to him, from then on out. Later on, they had to write what they thought of the music. And did he ever. There was something about him, she just didn't know what it was. Like a mixture of fine tobacco . . . you know how you find the good aroma left somewhere in a room where someone has been, she explained it like that to me. It went on like this. She gave out assignments. He sat in the back near the window, listening, writing what he saw, or sometimes, after it was all over, after it had finished playing, he'd turn a knob on, and tell her. She would look at his face through the glass, try to look at it, but he always looked down when he talked, he wouldn't look in her eyes. Then, one day she didn't put strangers playing the great music on, she put a tape of herself playing it. It was different, she saw him notice. It was only a short piece she played. He didn't say anything, he didn't turn a paper. He got up and walked out, forgetting to take the earphones off. He jerked them out of the sockets as he walked away. He left the room. The next time in class she played the regular music, but he cut in with his microphone and asked her would she play what she played last time. She did. He asked to hear it again. Before the class was over, they were looking each other in the eye. It took awhile. He looked up at her slowly, and looked at her and talked to her, and still not knowing it was her, but looking as if it was, he made her look down. What he said made her look down. Soon after that, she and Goll and some others were driving outside of town in the hills. They took the road up to where he stayed. It was fall. They heard some music going through the woods. It was coming from Dunbar's house, but there was no one there. Then they drove down the hill and she saw him cutting his firewood."

"I can tell you are about to tell a long story. One I want to hear, but one I can't stand to hear now. You are going to tell me about the woman and he, about death, about misery, about violence and a prison, and about more love and death. I want to know, Coover, I want to know like a man wants to know what there is after he dies, but I can't listen now. I can't hear it now. Before you go on I have to wait, wait for a dissolve to take place between what I've heard and what you are going to say. Do you understand?"

"Course I do, Ben Fallow. I understand more than you think, but I got to find my resting place. What you think, that I like going back like this. It tears me up. I guess the boy was living in a dream world about her. She introduced the others and her husband. It tore him up like a hollow point .22 shell. She saw him flinch. He walked off into the woods and cut on a huge tree all night. He quit coming to class, started staying drunk. Started hanging around in Smoking Cup, that's what they call niggertown there. I think he had a few scrapes with the law. He started acting mean, but he never really was. He got to where he'd talk if he was drunk, then he'd run back off into the mountains where his house was. Laid up there all the time. She sent him a note saying she'd fail him if he didn't come to class and write the papers, so he started going again. But he wouldn't talk, and he wouldn't write; he'd listen and fall asleep. I guess all he wanted to do was dream. It was in the winter then. She invited him to a party they were having. Maybe it was a Christmas party or New Year's, I don't know. Ben Fallow, it was those white people who give him that cocaine, he didn't get none of it in Smoking Cup. He walked all the way to the party in the snow. Of course, he came alone. He walked down off the mountain through the woods so he could stay off the slick streets. There was a full moon and he found tracks full of warm blood— it was hot cause the steam was rising off them like fog on the ponds. It was a rumpshot doe that had run herself into a barbed wire fence. There was a broken off arrow in her. He unsnagged the critter and slung it over his shoulders. He was half-drunk anyway. Hell, I'd a liked to a been with him when he knocked on the door of those folks house with his boot."

"He walked in with the doe over his shoulders?"

"That's what he done. He took it there cause he knew one of them shot her. I guess he'd seen him hunting in the woods. And who do you suppose it was?"

"The woman's husband."

"How'd you know?"

"I knew."

"He threw down the deer at his feet, and then he commenced to have a hell of a good time, just like he'd known them all his life. He drank and ate and danced and carried on. He was everybody's fool. Then he walked out the door, running towards the pond. The woman had just played the piano and sung something, and he took out across the field in his long black coat. And they went after him. It was snowing heavy and the moon was shining in his tracks. They all saw him jump in the pond. They saw him slide across the ice to the middle and beat it through with his fists and disappear. They all surrounded the pond, calling for him, no husband's wife letting them go in after him. A couple of the men tried, but the women wouldn't let them. They thought he was dead, they looked at the hands on their clocks. None of them knew he was a diver. He came up wet, dragging himself across the broken ice and snow, laughing to beat hell. That's when shit hit the fan. See, that woman had been there all along, wrapped up in a blanket, crying her eyes out. A wonder both of them didn't catch their death. She started beating him with her fists, screaming, and he let her. Then they walked off together towards a barn. A barn with a stove for the animals."

III

Coover forgot I was there. It seemed that he was remembering not for me but for himself. His eyes glowed like moisture in between the bottoms of our glasses and the black table. The sun was rising in the delta, thick as a country egg. And the broken pane of the moon drowned in the light skin of daylight, like a sliver that disappears somewhere in the vicinity of the fingers. I lost track of what he was saying, I did not want to hear. His voice was like a projector and my imagination a white screen overcome by the chiaroscuro of his story. The boy behind the counter, who had fallen asleep sometime in the night, suddenly rushed past us with a broom and, passing through the broken screen door like a mosquito, jumped off the porch, running after two butterflies going backwards in the morning air, trying to light on one another. Like dust in an old, high corner he could not reach, the boy swatted at the blue-black butterflies.

"He had never been to a concert before, not in his whole life. They had some great orchestra to come there, and the woman was to play the piano with them. The small auditorium at the college would not hold the people, so they let them have it at the old firetrap theater in the bad part of town. Most of the run-down churches and shotgun houses would have been condemned if they were in the white part of town. It was one of those real old places, the kind with all those balconies around the sides, and a place for the poor people and places for the rich . . ."

"The loges."

"Whatever you call them. I remember, he said they had a couple dozen old, colored women cleaning up the place. All the people with money and position sat on the bottom landing or in those, what you say, loges, and all the poor folks and students they sat up in the balcony. Lewis got him a ticket, but he wasn't about to sit in no balcony. He went down to a place and rented him a fine-looking set of clothes. Cept he got it all wrong. He went to one those places that rent costumes, not suits. They give him some fine threads, only they was for a long time ago, like in England or somewhere. He had a cape and cane and all that. What happened was this: all the colored folks just followed him, and he headed for those loges. They got all the special seats. Now this orchestra was from some place in Europe and the head of the college didn't want them to get the wrong ideas, so he jest let them stay. I can see all them niggers sitting up there now. I can see it like it was an old movie. They had wine and cold, fried fish, and coke. Those little snuff cans with the labels tore off was shining like lit matches he said. Some of the kids in Smoking Cup had stopped him and asked what was going on and what to do and what to wear. Lots of them had dressed up in choir robes. He said they were supposed to throw roses, so a bunch of them bad ones broke in a greenhouse and stole a bunch of them. The place was really stacked high. Then she walked in, and wearing a long black dress. Somehow the rumor had spread that the city and the college was going to donate the place to Smoking Cup folks for a nightclub or something after it was over, so they all went crazy, yelling and clapping. The white people sitting below turned around and looked up. I know they was wondering what on earth they was cheering for classical music for. They led out with her on piano and an old man playing Spanish guitar. They went crazy. She bowed with the old man after it was all over, and let her eyes wander over the audience. Then she saw where he was, where he said he'd be. You know, sometimes I think he might a been just a fool, just a fool in love; but she never thought that, not even looking at his suit, or listening to him talk. Her husband was sitting in the front row. He saw how she kept looking up at Dunbar, and Ben Fallow, he didn't like it at all. See, by then everybody knew he was black, and this here did happen awhile back, not that long, but long enough. Well, you can imagine what . . ."

"Not yet. Can you take me to that house you said was around here, the house he stayed in after he came back here?"

"If you really want to go there. The wasps probably took over in the eaves, but I'll take you if you want to see it. Close to here."

Spann wouldn't let either of us drive. He asked us where we were going and he'd have his boy, Pink Isral, take us. He'd have him put his bicycle in the back of my camper, and he'd drive us, then we'd have a way back. Coover told Spann we wanted to go to Dunbar Lewis's old place, and Spann looked at him like: *how come you want to do something like that.*

I thought I was seeing things when I saw the kid swinging over the bayou on a barge rope. He had on a little jock strap made out of rabbit fur and a coonskin hat. He was yelling like Tarzan. He landed in front of his father, out of breath, saying, "Lost that monkey again. Got to find him." But his father told him to drive us and not to worry about the monkey. He helped him with his bike and reminded him how to shift the gears. The boy got a jar with two dark butterflies in it and made me hold it while he drove. He didn't say a word to me except, "You need a bath. Both of you do!"

Sure enough, the wasps hummed like a high wire in their nests. I told Coover I had some bug spray in the camper. He pulled the boy by the ear and made me give him two dollars to run ahead of us and spray so we wouldn't get stung. Part of the old home was burned, and all that was left were ruins of columns. It was strange.

The tangle of an old chandelier hung in one room like a clump of roots. There were birds nesting there. There was a revolving, two-faced mirror in the hallway. Harmless dirt dobbers had flown their mud there for years. I saw a piece of an old quilt stuffed with newspapers. There were fishing nets, and hose, and a pair of lead diver's boots. Something was living in one of the boots but I did not want to know what. Wild blackberries were coming up all around the front porch swing. They'd stopped it from swinging in the wind. I was just ready to say something to Coover when I heard a loud scream.

"That's just Pink Isral beating his chest. He must have seen his monkey somewhere out there in the fields. Go on home Pink Isral," he yelled.

I saw a piano and a record player. Someone had taken the ivory keys, ripped them out.

"You want to hear what that woman played like? There some

old records in this chest, if they're still here. You want to hear?"

"Yes."

"See there what Spann's boy done to that Baby Grand? He thinks he's Tarzan and this is a great big jungle. Spann don't think so, but I think he's a little touched. He come in here with a crow bar one night an tore up all these keys. He put them in a cotton-sack and drug them back to Spann's place. He told everybody he was taking all the elephant tusks back to Africa. He said there was a sacred burial ground they must be returned to. Don't these chilluns have crazy ideas these days. Lord have mercy."

Coover had to spit on the record to get the dust off it. He turned on a knob on an old console set.

"You mean there's electricity here!"

"Always was, always will be. See, he just stole it off the power line. They never did know. That's how come half this place burned down. Lightning struck something, blew up some line and caught it all on fire."

The old set groaned, making a gurgling sound.

"Moisture in the tubes, Ben Fallow."

The first sounds of the old recording made a snoring noise. And then the piece of music. I imagined myself in the old theater that night in the winter when he first heard her play, when he first saw her perform. I seemed to have forgotten what I'd gone through since my wife's death, I no longer thought of her, just the young man, Lewis, and the woman whose name I hadn't heard Coover say. *After great pain a formal feeling comes,* a kind of effervescence of the spirits.

"So this is . . . this was Dunbar's room?" I asked Coover, walking into another room. He nodded.

"This here is where the poet lived. You see that painting?"

I couldn't believe my eyes. A large print of Gaugin's *Manao Tupapau* hung above a huge bedstead. The bed was facing the wall. There was writing, handwriting, on the ceiling. I tried to strain my neck, but I was too drunk to read it, I kept feeling in a swoon. I lay down on the bed and looked up at the writing.

"Ben Fallow, I feel like sleeping. I am going out to the truck and lie down. You can stay here if you want. Here, if that boy comes back you give him these back," he said, handing me the jar of fluttering butterflies.

There were empty bottles full of spiders; I heard Coover curse them as he walked out of the room. Although it was in a bad, small script, I could read it all. More or less:

A young girl is lying on her belly, revealing a part of her frightened face. She reposes on a bed covered with a blue pareo and a light chrome yellow sheet. There is a background of purple violet, strewn with flowers similar to electric sparks; a somewhat strange figure stands by the bed. Charmed by a form, a movement, I paint this with no other concern than to do a nude . . . In this somewhat daring pose, what can a young Tahitian girl be doing stark naked on a bed? Preparing for love?—This would be characteristic for her, but it is indecent, and I don't want it. Sleeping? —The act of love would be ended, which is still indecent. I see only fear . . . Having found my tupapau, I become completely attached to it and make it the motif of my picture, The Spirit of the Dead. *And the nude takes on the clothing of secondary importance. How does the girl imagine a ghost? She has never been to the theater, nor has she read novels, and when she thinks of a dead person, she can only think of that she has already seen. My ghost can only be some little old woman . . . A decorative sense leads me to strew flowers over the background. These are tupapau flowers, phosphorescences, indicating the ghost is thinking of you . . . And summing up, the musical element: undulating horizontal lines; harmonies of orange and blue woven together by yellows and violets and their derivatives, all lighted by greenish sparks. The literary element: the Spirit of a living girl bound to the Spirit of the dead. Night and Day . . . This genesis is written for those who always insist on knowing the whys and wherefores . . . Otherwise, it is simply a Tahitian nude study . . . The title* Manao Tupapau *has two meanings: she can be thinking of the ghost, or the ghost can be thinking of her.*

I slept until mid-morning when I heard something going past. A wasp orange as bittersweet stung me on the lip. Then there was a drum. The man in the tavern was walking down the road past the house, still beating the congas. Perhaps he was eating cocaine like Coover said. He was barefoot and had no shirt. I shut my eyes and wet my lip with my tongue. *And to think*, I told myself, *just days and nights ago, I thought I knew all there was to know.* The dark mourning cloaks had lived as long as they could; they died without air. I unscrewed the lid of the jar, and poured them out on the floor. The creatures and the atmosphere in the glass had formed a curious moisture within. Then I heard sniffing, like someone crying. A black, furry hand covered my eyes. I screamed like a woman. Me. I did.

I looked back through the iron bars of the bed at all the little boys laughing. Pink Isral had a five dollar bill rolled up and was sniffing white powder out of his palm. His monkey was crouched at my feet, smelling my toes. God, I don't know why I did it, but I kicked the beast in the teeth. It landed on the floor, the kids running to its aid, and Pink Isral calling me, "You bastard!" The monkey bled on the dust covering the floor; its blood flowed into an opening in one of the dirt dobber nests, and the blue wasp flew out beating the blood from its wings.

The monkey put its arms around Pink Isral's neck and whimpered. "I'm sorry, Goddamnit!"

One of them, who was sucking a lemon, gave me the finger, and they all backed out of the room. "Coover!"

11.

SURTEES' TALE

Surtees' Tale

When I told my friend, Enoch Hunnicut, that I was dead broke and about to lose my place near the campus just as my examinations for degree were coming up, he asked me, "Why?," then offered to share half of his tugboat, the place he lived on the lake. "It's a hell of a long story," I told him, explaining that some time ago I had received a letter with a picture of a small girl. It had come from a woman I'd never expected to hear from again, a woman who had always been proud and courageously independent, who was now writing me 'only as a last resort,' as she put it, and who began her letter 'Listen' and ended it 'So there.' "When she went anywhere with you, you felt like a bodyguard or a waiter; I don't think she made me feel that way, I made myself," I told him.

"Some of them like that, you know, they can talk some bad talk, thick as wheat; then they quiet, won't say a word. Cold, cold-blooded women, why they treat the way they do?"

"Look, Enoch, how long have you known me?"

"Long enough to know when you can make a fool out of yourself."

I took the snapshot out of my wallet and showed it to him. He held it up to the oil lamp and said, "Mighty fine. She looks just like her Daddy. You best watch those kind of letters, though. I've been played . . ."

"... for the fool before?"

He laughed like he'd been holding it in for some time, coming back at me with almost self-rehearsed quits. With his fist he beat over my heart to see if I was carrying a bottle. I was. He pulled us up two chairs and pulled back the make-do curtains on his large window to let in a little more light. The colder it got, the darker it got; and sooner. He sat in the chair backwards, leaning over towards me on its ladder, looking toward a large, new mirror I hadn't noticed until then. His hair had a bright sheen for that time of day, I thought, and he thumbed some of it away from his temples and moustache. He knocked on the round table, anxious for me to open up the bottle. I heard a pinging under us, coming from the bilge.

"Just that damn diver trying to find the leak."

"Too cold for me to be in the water," I said, trying to change the subject I had brought up, as he suggested I quit thinking about my empty savings account, and get back on the track with my studies.

"Don't worry bout the child," he said, "cause you done all you can, and the woman didn't want to get in touch with you in the first place, and you know she don't want nothing to do with you."

"True, true," I told him, as we killed the bottle in no time. I said I had better go pick up some things if I was going to stay, and he said we ought to borrow Spike's motorcycle and sidecar.

It surprised the hell out of me that Spike would lend us his wheels, especially when he knew that neither of us had licenses. He gave Enoch and I some goggles and pilot's caps and instructions on what to and not to do, then we were off. I drove and Enoch rode on my side. He found a bottle half full of wine in the glove box and he held it out to me. "Oh Cisco," he said, and I took it and said, "Oh Pancho!" Somewhere along the line he uncovered a tape player with two little earphones you plug in like hearing aids. The tape was some kind of African jazz, autoharps and drums and so on. We blazed through town, and I wondered if he shouldn't wrap himself up in a blanket. It was pretty brisk.

Surtees' Tale

I had the feeling he and I were on one of those cheap stages, one of those sets they throw up in the summer, but now all the tourists had gone, and we were near the ocean and the wind was blowing, it being near dark, and we were remembering the dancers that came that summer from another country, how they stubbed and splintered their fine feet on the unmatched tongue-and-groove planks.

"Watch where the hell you're going!"

"Shut up, I'm listening to this music!"

The landlord had put my books and clothes in a couple of boxes out on the steps. I threw the best box in the sidecar, and we took off again, this time for the boat, then I thought I'd best stop by the library — it looked like snow coming.

"Good thinking," Enoch said, "why don't you stop by the liquor store, too; you got to feed the spirit as well as the brain!"

"Don't have any money, man."

"Hell, tonight's on me: take a pass by there."

I pulled up outside a package store, one near campus, where the students go, and was about to cut off the engine, when Enoch pulled a little silver can out of his coat pocket, poured a hill of snuff out in the palm of his hand, sniffed it, then pulled out his lower lip and filled it from the can.

"Care for any? This here is cut good. I'll cut the mustard from the seed, and you can keep moving on the mountains."

"Don't mind if I do."

The shit hit me like air. Air in the loft of a haybarn at noon. He handed me a bill and told me to get whatever label I wanted. "The unbelievable cola," he said.

The man who waited on me in the liquor store was an acquaintance; I didn't know he worked there. I looked around on the cheap shelf and he pulled a slip of paper off the corkboard. He told me the order I placed on a foreign wine a few years back had to be picked up; it had arrived a year or so ago, and it couldn't collect dust any longer. I was embarrassed.

"Well, could you put it on the tab?"

"Hell, yes, anything for a friend. Anything to get rid of this crate."

"Thanks," I said, not believing anybody in that town would give me credit.

"That's one hell of a rig you're driving out there. You the nigger's chauffeur?"

"He's me guide," I said, but that didn't stop the fraternity boys and young businessmen from laughing.

The wooden case smelled like olives and seawater. A girl in a black sweater opened the door for me. I brushed past her with the case and webs caught on her wool.

"It must be awful cheap if a Fin will buy it. I got to tell a few folks about this wine," Enoch said.

"This is on me," I said, handing him his five back. "This drink has been waiting on me a long time."

God, Enoch looked strange. It was like being in England, or looking at a Rembrandt. All his clothes were thick and brown. His tweed overcoat, his turtleneck sweater, his herringbone pants, dark like bark, his two-toned shoes. "Cover up or you'll freeze," I told him.

A truck full of sanitary engineers went by. Some Negroes were hanging on the back and sideboards; some of them I'd seen before, and one called out to Enoch, "A meeting at Coldwater's!"

"Drive on, drive on, don't pay them any attention."

"O.K., I'm going by the library now, won't take me long."

"Sure. What the hell is this wine? You need a crowbar to unpack it."

"It came from Greece."

"So it did. I come from Hot Fork and I hadn't ever seen no wine this hard to open. Probably need a damn tool to get the corks out. What we need is an easy six for the road."

The garbage men swore at him. The smalltown block seemed endless. We waited for a train to cross. He got out and bought some beer in a joint by the tracks. I looked behind me at the students going into shops, bookstores, cafes, bakeries, and taverns; at the Goodwill Industries letting out their workers, the blind, the crippled, and so on, being helped up onto a pink and black bus; at the Frozen Dinner factory, workers coming off their shift, their white jackets and rubber boots soiled with turkey blood and grease; at the night shift of low-slung barmaids walking away from the stares of the men who dropped them off, and at the faces of the men who reach over and close the door and drive away alone. There was a poster on the window of a bookshop, a painting by Dante Gabriel Rossetti. "Wake up. Let's go ahead on after your books."

I pulled up between the Art and Music buildings, which floated like ships in the two moats constructed around them. I had to walk the thirty or so yards to the library steps, and the concrete seemed to give under my feet like the long plank of an unstudded floor. There was a bronze sculpture near the door; it was called CATERPILLAR, and there were plants on it. The last time I'd seen one hanging it was changing, or dying, one or the other. It was asleep in its own coffin-bed, eating leaves. I saw a middle-aged woman, very well dressed and loaded down with books, a teacher I think, scribble something on the sidewalk: *The Nooseless Gallows*.

I went downstairs, and the ship became more like a submarine. Two women were kissing in the stacks I was in. When they heard me, they stopped, and one buttoned her blouse and put on her coat and left. The other, the younger, went to a desk piled with papers, as if to go back to work on a report of some kind. I got the books I needed, stuffed them under my coat, and left.

When I got back to the motorcycle and sidecar, Enoch was staring up at something in the window, waving his hand. I could hear the music he was keeping time with, but I looked in vain for the image which held him spellbound.

"Sweet," he whispered.

"What?"

He pointed up to the light coming from an opening in the curtains of the Art building. Now I could see her; a tall, pale girl pressed against the glass.

"What in the hell kind of class is that?"

"Drawing, I suspect."

"I suspect I ought to do some drawing then."

We were laughing, dizzy, as if something carbonated was passing through our sinuses. A cold wind came around the building and I shivered. Enoch reached under the cowl of the sidecar and took out a black blanket. There was a hole for your head cut in the middle. "Put this around your neck," he barked, "unless you want to freeze to death."

I helped him out of the seat and his old knees buckled. "Goddamn the luck," he said.

"Just hold your horses," I said.

"Ain't got no horses. Don't they have a elevator around here we can use?"

"Yea, I'll carry you."

"Hold on, young man. Spike's got a mechanic's dolly down here. Find me some rope. I can stand but I can't walk good. I'll stand on it and you pull me."

I took the flagrope, got him steady, and took off. I even cut a length of rope to tie around the blanket. It was just dusk, and I was surprised none of the students noticed us. The place seemed isolated, unusual, like something was going on. Empty fountains, and gardens of sculptures, not even an odd one sitting in the cold, not even a bum off the train. The only sign of life was the back of the naked girl and the sound of the cellist.

We couldn't gain entry through the end glass doors, so I pulled him up to the theater door. He kept his balance by turning up one of the bottles of Greek wine. Our voices, as we whispered back insults and directions to one another, echoed through the empty gallery. I took off my shoes and loped down the long halls, Enoch coasting behind me. We got on the elevator. All we had to pass was the wing where they danced, the music room, then the upper room on the end.

"Hurry, she ain't going to be standing there, bare-assed, forever."

The door opened, a blind professor walked in. He smelled the liquor on our breaths, said students ought not to be allowed to drink in public. I think he was German. Enoch grimaced, motioned me quiet with his hands. He lipped the rim of the bottle like a drum fish. The door opened and I pulled him out. We picked up speed. The cut snuff was wearing off, but not the booze. I rounded the corner fast, looking back to see if he would make it, catch his balance and continue on down to the end of the hall, but he flew into an open door, took the wrong one by mistake and let go of the rope.

He disappeared. I heard a chorus of 'ahs' go up, ran into the room. The old dancing teacher had her back to the class and was giving a lesson in a difficult procedure; just as she turned her head over her shoulder, Enoch sailed in, goggles, long coat, ear flaps, and all. The poor woman dropped down on one knee. Later, they *told* me she had a stroke and it left her still from the waist down. They told me that.

But the dancers saved him, they caught him, kept him from crashing into the huge mirrors surrounding the room. There was a smile of adoration on Enoch's face as the girls lifted him up, held him close. He was particularly enchanted with a tall, black girl, whose yellow leotard was darkened with sweat. As they went to see about their teacher, I slipped in and pulled him out.

"Come on, Goddamnit, we don't have any business here. I'm liable to get kicked out." I looked to see if anyone was coming, if everyone was where they were supposed to be.

"Calm down, take it easy. Sure I belong here. I'm not going to scare them. I just want to look, man."

Someone was singing opera in another wing. We both leaned against the wall, catching our breaths. There was a small crack left in the door. "I'm going to look, one more time." I could see the tears fill up in his goggles. He was watching the girl in the motionless pose. "Funny how them Asian people look a little like us, ain't it?" he whispered to me. Little did he know what was going on, I said to myself.

We drove through the cool streets, past my old place, past the students walking from their hang-outs, then on down to the other side of town near the water, and we were cutting up, weaving back and forth, and we had the music played into our ears, and my papers blew out of the box in his lap and I didn't care. It was just perfect.

"Goddamn!" he called out. "Man the winch, the river's coming up, pull my house in!"

I ran into the side of an old wreck; it was lucky he didn't get thrown. The wind was up a little. I helped him draw in the cables and secure the tug. The catwalk was already floating eight feet away from the bank. We both got out of wind like you do when you're drunk and working. We unloaded my things and took them aboard.

"Remind me to tell you a story sometime," he said.

I wanted to talk and drink with him while he fixed supper, but he forced me to go into a room and study. I listened to him hum and cut things with a knife, being in no mood to read. I thought things were going pretty well, all considering. I looked in his shaving mirror. I looked in his drawers, in his closets, read a letter he had received. I even counted the money he had hidden in a slop jar.

Sure, I lied to him, I thought; but it would earn us both money, maybe even fame. I wasn't taking advantage of him at all, not at all. He was a born actor anyway. What would it hurt, I thought. I conjured up elaborte scenes, circumstances that I could capture.

I smelled his bed linens. I opened the curtains and looked out on the river. The low warning horns sounded like lauds chanted by monks who still had nuts. I took out my wallet and looked at the photograph of the child, then I wept. What a time to receive such a letter. Just now when I was ready to . . .

"You could stand a bath, you know that!" he yelled.

The wind was coming through the windows of the boat just as it did that night when I met her. It was whining. Christ, I didn't even have the two bits I needed for the beer I ordered. I think it was her first night there. And so she paid for it out of fear. We didn't know each other long. The first night we were together, that was the night she got pregnant. "My fucking luck," she told me a few months later. That first night we lay in bed and she asked questions about everything on earth, asked them like a child. I answered everything and nothing. I gave no suggestions. "Three lays a week for room and board. That's the last I'll ever ask you. I need a place to stay real bad. What about it?" she asked me, but by then I was dreaming she asked me that. When I woke, I smelled breakfast cooking. She was drinking vodka and juice. She must of fried a dozen eggs, and was sopping them up with stale light bread. I saw that most of her ring finger was missing just above the joint. She noticed me. "You're broke as I am, aren't you? I'm really going to take you, take you for everything you've got, aren't I?" I asked her what happened to her finger. She told me this story: "When I was sixteen or so I broke into this rich old lady's jewelry store. I'd been screwing her little, precious grandson, her heir . . . loom. I stole the ring and split. He was going into the Seminary. He ended up shooting himself, the old bitch drove him to it. She liked to make him dress up for dinner in their old, dark house. She was crazy. She liked to undress in front of him and all. That kind of crazy. She had this gardener, a real butcher. The fucker was a giant, about seven feet tall. If stray dogs or cats came on the place, she had the gardener torture them. I think she had a secret collection of some of the jewelry the Nazis made in the concentration camps. She owned everybody in the county. Anyway, I catch a slow freight out of Bergman, Arkansas. You know where that is? Really not a freight, just a spur that comes through there to pick up ties. The ties woods are around there. All the railroad ties in the South and the East come from there. I get on, but the boxcar has got more in it than lumber. It's full of caskets. Cheap, plastic coffins, that fasten like beer coolers. It was the train that moved the dead from the State Hospital, the nut-house, the old folks' place, and the criminal wards. That's the boxcar I hopped. I ride the thing to God knows where. It's cold, see. And I always carry charcoal on me just in case. I make a small fire in the boxcar. What do I know about fumes. I pass out. One of the caskets was empty. It fell over near me. They were light as coolers, I told you. Evidently, during the night, some drunk bum took me for a stiff, figured I rolled out on the floor. Naturally, the first thing he went for was the ring. He couldn't get it off. So he cut my finger off. I don't know why I didn't bleed to death. I got over it. I got even, too. I saw the ring in the window of a pawn shop in Paris. No, Paris, Arkansas. The man wouldn't tell me where the owner was. He was trying to cover for him. I stepped behind the counter. Took hold of his hand and put it down my pants. He told me. He swept at the Catholic church. I found him sober one Saturday evening, waiting for the priest for confession. I slipped in the little booth, listened to his shit, then reached through the bars with this hand. I could hear his heart tearing. It gave out like he was taking a dump. You wanna screw?"

We fixed some old, spoiled meat and by dark we were both down in the guts with food poisoning. "You and your fucking liver," she moaned all night.

We got well, but we didn't fall in love. All we did was go to the movies and stay drunk. When I wasn't with her, I was looking at people walking down the street. I was looking at them from my window. That's what I did at night. All that interested me was what the world was like outside the window that night. TURN YOUR SAD NIGHT INTO TOURS IN EUROPE is what the battered sign read over the pool hall. It used to be a travel agency. And there is a nest over it, outside my window, a woe, a hurt bird. "You keep wolfing down those apothegms of weightless love, we'll see where gravity is. This ain't the moon, this ain't space. You shithook. This snail's not going to leave another silver trail down your belly." She stole a twenty dollar bill out of my blue sock and split. I went to the store, put six cans of sardines in my overcoat pockets and walked the streets, eating. I smelled bad all week.

Going down the street one night my professor stopped me. He was in his car, and I saw he had another new cowboy hat on, another straw dog on his head. He told me to get in, asked me why I'd been out of class for a week. He drove me home, went up to my place with me. He didn't know live oak from ash, but he knew the mood floating in the room where a woman has recently departed. He said for me to come over to his house with him, that he'd give me a drink; we had a lot of important things to talk about, he said. He didn't shut up until morning when his wife told him to. He keeps buying straw cowboy hats, and his wife keeps burning them in the fireplace. There's got to be something wrong at home when a husband keeps wearing big hats and always carries a canoe on a rack on top of his car. I don't think anyone has ever seen him put it in water, but he drives it to class everyday. The more he went on, the more I knew I really didn't like him. I didn't respect him. I guess it was because his ideas appeared to be close to mine, but in reality their essences were light years apart. I couldn't stand the cosmetics, I wanted the simple mug, be it beautiful, false, or ugly. Soon I would fall from his graces, but I would do it in a way where he could feel guiltless; he didn't need anymore of that. Like the father who ignores his young brood because he knows he's dying. I became more and more aloof. I became plankton in the sea of those students who never return. Times we would pass in the hall, in the library, in the street, both of us proud and know it all. But I told him that night I'd just been leading him on. He'd suspected such. He was wounded, and I knew he'd known for some time, and I felt sorry for him. Most of the things I'd written, and told him, he knew I didn't believe. He knew I thought he was nothing; but nothing, friends, is more than most.

He said I'd led him into the shadow of the valley of death. He said I was unloyal. He saw through my effort to let him down easy, to make him hate me, hate me intellectually as well as truly. Perhaps I was too cruel. Maybe I should have filled him in from the start. But I think he really sought me out because he had faith that I would one day leave him with the truth, a stolen apple that will never rot. Then he told me, in the presence of his wife, that I was an angel who had come with a knife to dig out his heart. I remember reaching into my coat pocket and cutting my hand on the edge of the sardine tin. There was oil and fish and ooze all in my coat. I wiped my hand on his sofa. His wife called me "Scum" and I left.

"Chicken livers and onions," Enoch said, bringing in the tray.

"Can I tell you something Mr. Hunnicut?"

"Not before I tell you I know you wasn't studying about studying. What's wrong, don't you like it here? Not good enough for you? Can't you concentrate?"

"I feel like shit, like I'm taking you for a ride. I've got something I want to shoot, but I've got to tell you something personal before I level with you. Listen, I have the strange feeling I'm being watched. Even now. But I've had this feeling all my life, but it doesn't affect my actions at all. I act in spite of it all. It's not like a feeling of God, either, it's like there is a cameraman out there. I tell you . . ."

You got to settle down, you've been through a lot lately. You don't mean you do things to spite . . ."

"No, *in* spite . . . I'm going to tell you something. I don't want you to take it wrong. Everything I told you is the truth, but not the full truth, Enoch."

"Hush, boy. I ain't got time for that dogshit. Eat and study, then let's go over to the place."

"There's something you don't know. Some other people are in on this . . ."

"Everybody is in on everything. Shut up and eat before it gets cold."

I ate the chicken livers, the boat swayed under me. The drums full of concrete that keep the quays in place, they call them dead men. I hoped the dead men held us secure. He brought in the crate of wine. "We sure as hell won't need this cheap shit. I don't think anybody would touch it. I believe I'll get rid of these bottles in the closet somewhere and let you use the case for a shelf; I see you already put one book in there."

"What do you mean?" I said, licking the sauce off my plate. "Man, that's good wine; I'll turn a shelf out of it after I drink it; one of my books must have fallen in there on the cycle."

"Well, you sho tore this one up. The library ought to make you pay for it." He handed me a sheaf of papers sewn up with black thread.

"This isn't a book, this is someone's papers. This isn't mine. How the hell did it get here; not unless I accidentally took it from the library. Don't tell me it was nailed shut in the case all along."

He made a sandwich out of the burnt, purple onions and liver scraps. "Wasn't that a sweet girl dancing in the room? What was she, Chinese?"

I examined the old manuscript. It smelled like wood with dryrot. Of course, I couldn't read the Greek characters, but the signature looked familiar. I'd seen it somewhere. I went through my box of books. There it was, I found what I was looking for. I compared the embossed signature on my volume to the one on the manuscript. I've got to be dreaming, I thought. How could I run into such luck. "Do you know what this is, Enoch? Do you know what this means? We've ended up with a manuscript by a great . . ."

"Don't go telling everybody about it now, keep it to yourself. Pipe down. There might be some secrets in it. Some spies might be looking for it." He was drunk.

I laughed. "Not hardly. This means . . ."

"Damnit to hell," Enoch yelled, taking a broom to a quick, dark critter. "Scoundrel eating my eggs."

The animal didn't even startle me, I was so overwhelmed by what I'd found. "Enoch, this means I can give up this whole pantomime. This eclipses what I'm doing. I can forget about making money for awhile. Do you understand how much this is going to bring us?"

"I dare you to come back again you bastard!" He wasn't listening to me. "Give a rat a place to stay and the son-of-a-bitch is liable to eat you out of house and home!"

"Listen, Enoch, I've got to get in touch with someone."

"You too drunk. Let's go to Coldwater's place."

"Just let me write this letter—to an old teacher friend. I'll just be a minute. God, I can celebrate."

He went to his bedroom and combed his hair. "I'll take a few extra bucks in case anybody has a mind to shoot dice!" I saw him pick up my wallet, slip a five into the pouch. He looked at the picture of the child. The past started seeping into the present like water in a cracked, earthen crock.

"Cute little girl you got!"

Immediately, my thoughts went back to the morning I walked out of the professor's house, gnats on a scab. I needed sleep. I go back to my house where I know the girl with one finger missing is gone. I typed a letter to the professor. I tore it up. I type it again. I would deliver it to him in person the next day; I would sit in his study, Bellerphonic, while he read it. I tore it up.

The house seemed bare, and yet in order. Strange there weren't a woman's things scattered all about. The place looked too clean, too tidy. I got into bed. She was there, I felt her, I thought. I put my leg and my arm around her and dropped off to sleep.

The phone rang. It was another day. It was my teacher. Lay off, he said. Calm down. Come back to class. I told him a lie, hung up. I turned over and flinched. It wasn't Lucy, it was his wife, the seven years of bad luck.

She pointed a pistol at me, "You need a drink."

She told me to get a bottle out of her overnight bag. Those

seconds went through my mind like frightened minnows. I turned the bottle up and looked her in the eye.

"Kill it," she said.

I was shaking. She stuck the gun under my chin. "I'd love to blow your brains out," she gritted.

Enoch chased the critter around the tugboat with a broom. I finished the note to my teacher. Got an ancient, dusty stamp from Enoch's cuff link and thought to mail it on the way to Spike's.

"Come on, boy, I say the night is young and cold as boots under a warm bed. Here, now, you give me my stamp back. I've been saving that, it's got sentimental value. We'll get some kid to ride his bike over to the man's house, he'll do it for a dime.

"We left the boathouse, then, against my wishes, and without the manuscript. "What if it burns, what if it sinks, this storm might not pass, it's too much of a chance . . ."

"Forget it," he sneered.

I could light snow in the heavens and I worried it would fall off the roof and weigh the boat down. I stepped down on the starter of the cycle; it hit the first lick. Enoch gave me another palm of snuff. "This stuff will give you plenty of warm shade," he said.

I sucked it all up my nose. "I'm in a hell of a good mood. I might even borrow five on what the future might bring."

"Now you talking!"

We headed across the tracks and down the road to Coldwater's place. The snow melted, flying into my goggles. People looked at us as if we were the ghosts of fools. I thought about Lucy, how she cast a shadow like a tombstone, made shade like a tree.

We went into the place, and the same old man with the sprigs of mint told us time. Everyone was drinking Cold Duck which had just been given away, listening to old hot lick jazz. There was a waiter in a cut-away white jacket who kept dancing with a fifth on a platter; he never spilled a drop. Most everyone was dancing, or chatting, or gambling near the huge fireplace. You could drive a bulldozer through Coldwater's fireplace.

"I can see myself getting caught again in a place like this, getting kicked out of school," I told Enoch.

"Never mind," he said.

Coldwater looked like a captain and his white house became a ship. I remember: The band is dressed in white suits. The leader has on tails and a top hat. He plays tenor sax and wiggles around the room. There is a quivering chandelier hanging down over the garbage man's crap table. He was the one on the back of the truck in town. Spike was glass-eyed. He had a handful of cash and wouldn't let go of his turn. Women helping men up the stairs, that wind like a snake after a nest in the top of a tree. The hors d'oeuvres are pig feet, baked goat and apples, young brains and hard-boiled eggs. There are lots of peanuts and onions. A fat lady with a cane is eating peanut butter and jam on toast. Either a kid or a midget is walking around in a turban, bringing matches and pills. Enoch gives him a dollar and my letter and tells him to deliver it. I see a woman alone at the top of the stairs, it couldn't be the professor's wife. She is standing beneath a very large painting called *The Mystery of Linda Chase*. She is smoking weed in a long holder, looking at me as if I were piss on the rug. I look at the rug. It seethes in and out like a nest of water snakes.

I thought at the time, as soon as I heard from the professor I would tell Enoch the secret. When the news was out about the strange bottle of aged words we found, those people who made it a habit of passing by me in the halls and on the streets as if I were not there, they would take great pains if I would only grant them a few minutes of my time. There would be invitations from most of the universities, here and abroad — not to speak of the money, the loot of fame. I hadn't enough money to buy a rubber or an envelope or a beer, but soon I could go into business, selling ideas like pork chops. I would buy a bookstore maybe, and deal only in works concerning finance and high art. Perhaps I'd buy Coldwater's place and hire everyone to entertain my guests, or a farm to provide an endless supply of eggplants. I'd invest in a female singer, one who wrote her own lyrics. Enoch bumped into me; he had a leg of pink goat.

"Come on upstairs with me, boy; they's a white woman up there that loves minnows. A couple hundred live shiners up there. She lets you dip them out on her, watch them flap and die. Coldwater don't miss a thing does he?"

The rooms were huge as clearings in a forest. Tall, abundant plants marked every corner, and there were air ferns, I took a silver dish of olives and walked towards the fireplace where one other, solitary guest was biding his time, gazing into the flame, his hand on the mantle, lost in the reckless party. It was perfect. I looked around the room to see where my people could possibly be hiding, wondering how in hell they got Coldwater to go along with it. The Negro near the fire looked at me; 'just another one,' I thought I could see him telling me with his eyes. I reeled from the cut snuff Enoch had given me. I felt like a diver, amaurotic under water, effervescence originated in the roots of my hair and ascended to the ceiling. Was it look that took me to this costume ball, or was it contrived; perhaps the old clothes were the best they had; they might not be costumes at all.

I looked at the back of the quiet man standing beside me. He wore a long, green velvet coat and a strange Bush hat. On the little finger of his right hand he had a jade ring. He chuckled to himself as the dancers and musicians formed a line and writhed through the room. picking up stray guests here and there. The man standing over the fire seemed unmoved though, even when the leader, the saxophonist in white tails and top hat, passed by us, wobble-kneed, knocking the former's hat from his head. He only rose his hollow stem glass of Duck to the guests, toasting them in a careful, silent way. The man looked familiar, and yet I couldn't place him for the life of me. It is odd the way we carry on with friends and strangers. There are those we see often, from day to day, and we never think twice about them, even when they burden us with cables of bad news, then there are those we are hardly acquainted with at all, seldom ever seeing them, but we always know them, even in dreams we know them, remembering their faces above others. Yes, finally the Mass of the small time and no money was over, and I would be going, soon, in peace. By now, the boy or the midget had taken the letter to my teacher's house, delivered it. And the check I sent Lucy, she was eating off it and the child had a sailor dress or an animal or paid bill at the doctor's. Something to sleep with, something so you can sleep. Yes, and I soon, too, I would be seeing the rushes of this film, like Moses in a basket. These strangers to you would be fluttering guests in a matter of months. And that stack of stinking paper on the tug, that was my face card in the hole. Sure, I had to tell Enoch what was going on, but the others were going along with it so it couldn't be all that bad an idea. And with change of luck and fortune imminent, he would forgive me, I know. Yes, while everyone else in town was loafing on the job, the labor of building their ships of death, I was nailing way into the night.

I had accumulated, by then, a handful of pits from the olives. I threw them in the fire. They hissed, and the Negro in the long, green coat, whose head I just noticed was bald, turned and said, "How do you find us?" in a deep voice, as if he were speaking from the bottom of a river. I was startled. I knew where I'd seen him. He was the mortician. They'd taken his medical license away, and now he was an undertaker. A loner like me, but very wealthy.

"Care for some Cold Duck?"

"Thanks," I said.

"You know, most of the students are leery of Coldwater's place. I think they worry about violence or police. May I ask you if you have some kind of motive for being here, other than for a good time?"

"At first I had a reason, but not anymore. Now I'm thinking about something completely different, I'm just having a good buzz."

"That's all well and good. Shall we move away from the fire?"

"Yea, it's getting a little warm in here."

We walked over to a little hallway, a common entrance to the place, usually the way men came in when they were just getting off work. There was a corkboard up for messages and items of interest. There was a picture of Christ kneeling in Gethsemane and next to it a notice about a dog named Twilight that would stand for stud at ten bucks a throw. "A strange collage?" he asked me, smiling.

"Yea."

"You seemed to know that woman upstairs. You seemed to avoid her."

"They ought to lock her up. She's crazy as hell. She really has a lust for blood. Do you know she's actually sent two people to their graves, and gotten off because of her husband's reputation and . . ."

". . . By reason of insanity? Yes, I know."

"She scares me worse than the Hell's Angels."

We heard a scream upstairs, a black man screaming like he was singing. Then the kid in the turban slid down the bannister. He saw me and came towards us, but he said something in Enoch's ear before he got to us. Enoch looked at me, and nodded, as if to say all's taken care of. The boy told me, "The lady upstairs, she say she dares you to come up and see her." There was snow melting all over his cape. Just then, my side of the room shook with the laughter of a big woman. A mirror near the window swayed and from underneath it fell a dead moth. "Excuse me," I said to the undertaker, while I pressed my face against the cool glass, looking out into the street, the snow, almost blue, falling beneath the lamps. Looking back over my shoulder, the bandleader had his head thrown back, eyes shut, shaking a finger, and the big woman was sucking oyster off the half-shell. I stumbled towards the fireplace, where the kid was roasting marshmallows on a forked stick. The mortician was popping them into his mouth. I felt my knees giving out under me, as if I hadn't quite got my sea legs.

"Alright, Goddamn you brass-assed bitch!" I called out, looking all over the room for her, past Enoch and the undertaker, past the bandleader and the paintings *The Mystery of Linda Chase* and *The One I Call Mistress to the House of I*, then I fell down on my knees in front of Coldwater's fireplace.

II

I came to my senses a week later; if I had awakened before then, I no longer remembered doing so, nor did I remember any dreams, only those which I've always carried with me like a medal: I was a boy. The cool weather had come to our house in the forest and I was cleaning the soot from the stovepipe. A man in a blue suit came walking down the road, leading a mule with a crate on its back. The man tipped his hat, asked to see the man of the household. I told him my father had been dead three years. He asked if there were an older brother, and I said no, just a sister and my mother. I told him my mother was in the fields, gathering food. He led the mule the way I pointed. My mother did not come in to fix dinner, neither did she come for supper. I went to bed hungry. The next morning I awoke to the pleasant sounds of the porch swing creaking, I was content, too happy to rise out of bed. She is back, I thought, for I smelled good meat cooking and I heard the visitor's voice. He was a bookseller, he told her, he had come to show us many volumes of *The Book of Knowledge*, but it was not my mother's voice that answered back. It was my sister's. I lay there, listening and sleeping. After a long while, I heard no more voices, only the lullaby of the swing. I got out of bed and went to the window and looked out onto our large, white porch. My sister's back was to me and he faced towards me. My sister was sitting on his lap, straddled. Her underpants were on the floor. He had his hands around her dark hips, and I could see the shadows of her bosom cast on the ground. She was stroking her hair, pulling it back, as if she were looking in the mirror. His boots were next to the crate of books. The cat was smelling them. I remember her dress, light as a pillowcase and made of the same print. Her legs moved like she was riding her bicycle — those are the other times I had seen flashes of her underneath. Written on the wooden crate were the words: The Book of Knowledge.

All the hair from my face and head had been shaved. I did not recognize my room as one in a hospital. I turned to a bedside table, looking for any kind of note or letter, some kind of writing congratulating me. Whatever had happened, a week was sufficient time to set things in motion. There was nothing. My head felt like a monastery belfry. Certainly, they didn't include this in the plan, this couldn't have been a part of the agreement. There must have been an accident, I thought, looking out from the second or third story window at a field of yellow flowers. A week is not the only thing that's passed, 'there are flowers,' I said to myself. I pushed open the window. 'Spring.' The sun was brighter than wet eyes.

Except for the huge bed and desk, the room was bare, as if it had only recently been called on to take in a stranger. There was a sound at the door. A timid child walked in, holding an envelope. It was she, already older than the picture. She held out the envelope, shutting her eyes with shyness. It dropped to the floor, then she ran away. I leaned over and picked it up. It was from the professor, and dated midnight of the following day I wrote him. It read:

Dear Infidel,

Obviously you were drunk, or God knows what, when you sent the note. Of course, I was glad to hear from you, even at that hour and by such a strange messenger, but I was very sorry with your conduct and what you attempted to perpetrate on me — I didn't know you had gone that low. Although I am not altogether certain of your intentions, your *motives*, there being complications, I do feel, at this time, it is a fair assumption that you intended this hoax at my expense. And, I'm surprised and angry that you involved my poor wife in all of this.

You should feel satisfied to know that your ploy was fully working until I found you out. I made a fool out of myself, but I intend to see to it that you never have the chance to make even that out of yourself. The same hour I received your letter, I ventured out on icy roads, down near the river to niggertown, and proceeded to wait for you until the early hours of the next morning. Then, Enoch, your landlord, or friend, or whatever, told me you'd left the party somewhere around midnight and you hadn't returned. He said you were very drunk. He was drunk himself. When I asked him about the manuscript you said you'd found in the wooden crate of wine, he said he didn't know what I was talking about. I tried to be more specific. He took me to the back of his tugboat, and pulled out a paperback copy of Greek songs. He asked me if that was what I was looking for.

So you've had your fun, but you have caused my wife and myself great pain. I am not really sorry about what happened to your friend, but my wife had never been to that part of town before and she was afraid those people were going to do something to her. You know how they are, obviously. I will take every measure I can to see to it that in this profession your name will be mud from here on out. In my book, you will never see yourself amount to anything, not a thing.

Ivan Lubenkov

Now what in hell is he talking about, I thought. Enoch was probably too drunk, too stoned, he said he was. Could I have told Enoch about the film crew and could he have gotten mad over it? Yes, he probably took offense, left the party early like me, and decided to get even. That little kid in the turban probably had something to do with it. Old Hunnicut has the manuscript in his boathouse and he's just waiting for me to come get it. That professor will see, they all will. But when was the last time I saw

Enoch, I thought. And what is the date of today? I looked on the back of the envelope, looked in the desk, got a pencil, and wrote:

Dear Enoch,

Just came to. What's all this with the professor? If you don't know, please read the other side of this. We've got to rush, we've got to set the picture straight for him. By the way, what happened to you, get busted? For that matter, what happened to me? I *think* I'm in good hands.

Now, please let me explain everything. If I tried to tell you before, you wouldn't let me, I was too far gone. Get in touch with the man on the other side of this letter and give him what we found in the wine crate. Please. Now here it is, I'm putting it on the line. The movie was to my benefit money-wise, since I told the director I would see to it he got enough real-life footage of you and your way of life — with no bullshit, but I know you could profit from it too. You would get a cut of the gate, become, in a sense, immortal, and might even land a few jobs acting. Look at all the stars discovered in documentary films. Those people can make more in one day than you and I can make in a year, and that's no lie. So, you can see my position. I'm sorry I had to string you along like that, but we had to be realistic. Goddamn, but Coldwater's house and that rat and that manuscript, that might be more than most can handle. Sorry, but I had to do it. Believe it or not, getting that letter and picture from Lucy, it really made me think about what I was doing. Everything happened at once. I worried a lot about that; I didn't want to take advantage of our friendship. Anyway, what we changed by this film is for the good in the long run. And Lucy and the girl, that's good. And my getting back in touch with Ivan, so is that, especially since he needs something like that. He's really worse off than you or I or Lucy. We just hurt our bodies, our souls, but he's got pinch, the hard ache in his mind. Notice I didn't say a damn word about his wife. She's strange as snow in August. And, you know, what we found in the box will be appreciated by many, the work of a great, dead man. I'm willing to share everything, cut it right down the middle. You know that big yacht you said you liked, you might even be able to buy it. (Sorry this handwriting is so small.)

You know, now I realize what it feels like to be made a fool of, and what's going through my head at the moment is we are liable to get jilted by that director and his film crew, we just might be fools in the long run if we don't do something about what he's doing. You and I never needed a movie before, just a little cash and some more credit, so what is your opinion? I'm changing horses in midstream, but what do you think? Maybe they're trying to pull one over on us. Now that I think about it, I revise the above, maybe it's because of my shaved head and circumstances, but I feel like I'm on stage, a little suspicious, you know what I mean? I'll tell you what, old friend. Nobody's going to make a movie out of you. It's horrible to be a victim of circumstance, a victim of con artists. Everything I told you was true, I just didn't take it far enough. Please let me hear from you, or come visit. Don't worry about that movie either, I'm going to get rid of it. I intend to rise off this bed, put on my clothes, go to the college, and destroy it. I'm not going to let anybody make dust of dirt. However, please don't follow my example in regards to what we found in the wine crate. That's something different. You wouldn't catch me burning the snapshot of my little girl. That is genuine.

Your eternal friend,
Surtees

The perfunctory act of reading one letter and writing another soon after—which meant a lot to me, had exhausted me. The best thing I could have done was call some painter to catch me lying there, forever, some artist who was not afraid to follow Vermeer. It always seems that some smart-aleck character off the streets is always trying to be close with us, always giving us an embarrassing gift which we are afraid to open. I suppose it is like this: Once, long ago, in the early fall, I was sent out to cut stove wood. I heard other boys hunting, shouting, their favorite dogs barking through the hills. Off in the distance, the sun was coming through a break of timber just as it was coming through my window in the spare and simple room, and it was hitting the morning fog and an intricate spider's web. I listened. I could hear the boys, and I could hear people singing hymns in the white church below in the valley. What the spider had done was beautiful. When the church let out, some of them had come up the hill on their way home. I stopped an old truck and told them about the enormous, wonderful web; I asked the grandfather what kind of spider would build such a web. He laughed, and said, "Go look at it again." I did. It was a strand of new chickenwire. Later, I was to find out that over the years many a boy thought he had seen the same thing, there was someone who never allowed the wire to go to rust, they always replaced it with some new. Then I heard more shouting, but no dogs. I listened. One of the boys had shot his companion in the face. "He looked like a fox," the boy contended throughout his manhood.

There is a tale told around here about a fox who knows everything. However, the hedgehog, who only knows one thing well, survives; but he endures without knowing what the fox knew. A great man—but not as great as that Greek whose handwritten book I found—has said that all roads are long, and at the end of those roads what concerns us is how we walked them. This may be so for those who travel for the sake of travelling, but not for me. Oh yes, I've learned from walking, but it is what I find on the journeys that makes me step. How I would have liked to have talked to someone that day. My conscience was like a clear night, just falling. But every star, no matter how dim, was a vivid reminder of my guilt. My child appeared in the room again, still very timid. She had a rose in a drinking glass. I took the rose out of the glass, and drank the water. "Where is your mother?" I asked, while she smiled at me. She looked down at the floor, making her lips disappear. I handed the letter to her, "Give this to your mother, she'll know what to do with it." I went to sleep.

I woke up in the dark, in a cold sweat. The moon was up. Everything, light and dark, humiliated me, reminded me of myself. First the stars had blistered me with a pox of guilt, and then the moon drowned them out, festering at my feet like a chancre. A dog howled, as if someone had kicked it; it didn't howl out of hunger or thirst or love. I remembered Enoch's dog, the one he had to put out of its misery, holding its jaws together so it could no longer breathe, its young lungs filled with the phlegm of distemper.

I found myself, the next morning, listless, sitting in a straw rocker before a stone fireplace. There was a kettle of soup on the grate. My eyes hurt to look at anything. I half closed them, inhaling the wood smoke. It was a nice, crisp morning, with just enough wind to keep you from taking off your wraps. There, to my right, next to a wooden chest, was the child. She was eating ice, a plain snow cone without flavoring. At the time, I guessed that it was nearly nine o'clock in the morning. The room, clean but cluttered, was filled with spring flowers in all kinds of make-do vases. I could see webs and dust, but the house was fresh, as if someone had just moved in. A mirror was hanging, at a downward slope, over the fireplace. I saw my pale face, its blue shadow, my bare face that I had forgotten. Near the row of windows was a large, blonde library table. There was absolutely nothing on it, nothing. I looked out at the water. Again, I wish a painter had been there. This time, an archaeologist of light, Hopper.

The child got up off the floor and curled up in my lap, as if someone had directed her. The fire was just warm enough to take the chill from the morning. A beautiful clock, evidently just unpacked, was standing behind me; it wasn't running. There seemed to be nothing but a moist light around the room. And the child's hair smelled like smoke. A breeze rustled outside, and I wiped the drool off my chest which had dropped from her lips. She was asleep. There was a silence too quiet to be called silence, as I doubt

I would have heard anything had I been listening. I had restitutions to make with people, I thought, and they would all be simple, faithful acts. I felt absolved. Surtees reprieves himself. Lucy walked into the room with sweat on her brow and dirt on her hands and knees. She carried a bowl of blueberries. "They're wild," she said.

Later in the day, she helped me out to the garden. The yard was in a mess; someone had let it go to seed. "I'll have this hog pen looking great in no time," she said.

"What . . ." I got out.

"That's not the scaffold, it is a beginning on a gazebo. I've got the platform done, but I'll need your help on the rest, the beams, and so on."

I sat on the platform and she pulled weeds nearby. Unfinished, the thing was almost akin to those kinds of things the ancients did whenever they were inspired, some homemade tabernacle, some tombstone to remind all that the creator was not yet dead.

"There's probably a universe of questions you want to ask me now," she said, buttoning her blouse. "You can tell I've changed. And I'm not the kind who says that every other month. I have."

I remained silent, not the creature of pride, but the animal of senses; because I was reluctant to interrupt the last few hours of bright light in the afternoon. She went on working through her rows. Then she brushed back her hair, pinned it and wiped the sweat off her forehead, dirt on her fingers, and said, "Did you ever think . . ."

"No," I broke in, "before we get to us, did you get the letter to Enoch, it's very important; it could be important to us?"

"No."

"Why not?"

"Enoch can't read it now. He's sick again. Spike told Coldwater to come over here and tell me. I didn't read the letter, but I didn't send it. Please don't get mad. Things have gone all wrong, they're not what you planned, but it isn't your fault. You're going to know sometime, you're bound to, but it isn't up to me to tell you. Not now, and I promised."

"He ought to get this note, though. So he'll know something, so the professor will know something. YOU'VE got to see that they . . ." I raised my voice.

"Quiet, you're getting upset. You can't afford to. Calm down."

"What do you mean? And listen, why didn't you get in touch with me before? Why the picture just the other day? By the way, when was that picture taken? She's grown so."

"I *mean* there are a lot of questions I will answer."

"Look," I said, "there are more answers than questions, so why don't you begin?"

"Alright, First, I know all about the movie. I know something about it you don't know, but it's not up to me to tell you. O.K."

"O.K. So you know some business details I'm not up on, go ahead."

"You're not giving me a chance."

"I'm sorry. It's just I'm so goddamn curious. What is going on? I thought I was running this show."

"Here goes. You ran out the door of Coldwater's house in the snow, fell on the ice, and split your head wide open. That was some time ago. I guess it was chance, but I'd just blown into town. Decided to pass by your place. Saw some other folks had moved in, so I went down to the bar where I used to work. This spade dude asked me if I wanted to go to a party. I asked if he knew you, he said sure. I said I'd go with him if he'd let go of me as soon as I saw you. The guy was real nice about it. Stayed at the party awhile, asked around for you or Enoch. They said you'd both split. Went to his boathouse. Found him. He'd already talked to that high and mighty professor of yours. Enoch had come back to his place, worried about you. He had a run-in with the professor, but soon after that his wife paid a visit. She tried to kill Enoch with an oar. She really beat him up bad. No one knows why, not really. Enoch was holding his side when we got to him, but we didn't know how bad it was. Later, we found out he had broken ribs and a punctured lung. He was cold and wet, still drunk; he just kept worrying about you, saying he was afraid he'd lost your friendship

Surtees' Tale 147

on account of this movie. He kept saying the whole thing was his fault."

"His fault?"

"Enoch told me all about the movie, and the manuscript; but I don't have anything to do with *that*. He said you were worried too much about what you did to your friends, he said you ought to start looking out for yourself more, what your friends could do to you. Then, he told me what you'd told him about us."

"Oh, yea?"

"I was crazy to leave, Surtees. But I didn't want to be a spider-woman. I was mean in those days, mean. I didn't want you to feel you were obligated to me. I hate that."

The birds were digging holes, eating things out of the garden. She was crouched down, about to cry, I think, shading her eyes with a silver trowel.

"The guy I was with got hold of Spike and Coldwater and we were going to take Enoch to the hospital. That's when we found you. The car wouldn't start, and the roads were getting really bad. We didn't want to move you much, so Spike woke up the Fish Man. We used his wagon and mules. We put both of you in the back and covered you with blankets. It was funny. Enoch was in pain, but he couldn't stand all those half-frozen catfish moving around. He kept cussing at them. The baby and I rode in the back with you. We didn't worry too much about Enoch, he seemed alright. It was you who were close to death. You lost lots of blood. It was really close with you for awhile, Surtees. Christ, I didn't drag that kid all the way back here to go to your funeral. Well, Enoch has had a relapse. Up until a few days ago, he came by every day and sat with you. I thought everything was going fine, then . . ."

"Hunnicut, you don't find anybody better."

"He'll pull through, just you don't try anything crazy."

"I feel like there's this infinity of obligation I have to everyone, my friends, I owe . . ."

"That kid in there, but you don't owe anybody anything. You've got six months of summer and sleep. You've got time to dream, not suffer. Remember that kid whose grandmother's ring I stole. Well, all that is settled. I had to serve a little time, but listen to this. In the will, the kid left me a little money, not much but enough to get us started. What do you think?"

"I don't know."

"You ought to know this, people care about you. If you still think you're a goddamn stone, then there's other stones around you, moss on your belly now. That plane you're in, where you think, it's like the mirror perilous, but you aren't afraid of the truth like everybody else, hell no, you don't even care, you just don't want your mug to show up there. You want to be gone. You don't want footprints, not even a trace. You can't un-exist yourself. You've got to forget what you can't remember."

"What?"

"In a few days you'll be strong enough to go see Enoch. He'll tell you about all this movie business. Now, listen. I've got this place and a job. I want you here, I don't want you fucking it all away."

"You're telling me everything?"

"Everything I can. I don't know what you've done since I last saw you, maybe Enoch does. He told me a little. How about some supper, Surtees? A real one. I've got to work tonight, but as soon as you're well, let's get lit, let's go down to the lake and talk all night, then we can go to a good movie."

"I've got to do some kind of work."

"Sure, but get well first. If you feel better, just cut some firewood. Unpack some books or something. Just don't think."

"What a day, Lucy."

"And, yea, the kid's name is Judy."

"Yea, I like that."

That night, after she had gone to work, I slipped out and went down to the lake. I got in a skiff and motored to the city limits. I walked to the college. The theater department door was locked.

I broke in. I heard music and saw the blind professor standing in the entrance to the dance floor. He must have been friends with the old dancing teacher, I thought. No one was around, only works and announcements and notices and cancellations, nailed up on a board. I do not remember what music was playing as I walked down the hall towards the editing room, but I heard it; I heard it even as I opened the three cannisters of mockery and deception and exploitation. I thought it strange that all three lids were marked with my name and not Enoch's. He'd never been made a fool of, I thought. A chance at greatness isn't worth the price of being a fool. Without looking at one frame, I took the three spools downstairs to the gallery where the coals of the fireplace were still glowing. No one was around, only the old blind professor and some persistent musician, and what the great artists had left behind, and not even that, because they were prints hanging there along side of unfortunate originals by those I'd never heard of.

They exploded when I threw them in the fire. They burned like the aurora borealis and St. Elmo's fire put together. "What are you doing?" the blind man said. I must have been losing my mind, because he looked like that bookseller that came to see my mother and sister on our place, our place in my dreams.

I ran off to the boathouse to see if I could find anything else, hoping to run into Spike and borrow his sidecar and cycle. But I saw all of them out in front of Coldwater's place. Lucy was there, she was holding the baby. "Everything's taken care of," I told them. "Don't a soul worry."

This is what Lucy said: "Enoch died."

"Bout half an hour ago," Coldwater said.

They were about to tell me more, but I left on Spike's bike for the boathouse. I cut the cables with an ax and ripped up the gangplank. The motor on the stern still had a link or two left in it, so I started it and headed out into the current, letting it drift towards the chain of locks and dams. Maybe I'll wind up at Lucy's on the lake, I didn't know. In the bow, where he kept his liquor stashed, there was a steering wheel, but I found it spun freely, it controlled nothing. I guess some of them called out after me, but Lucy made them stop because she knew I'd end up wherever I ended up. There it wās, his note, in the crate of wine, and it smelled too, like seawater and olives.

Dear Surtees,

Hope you're in better SPIRITS by now. Get it? Hell, boy, you're an old dog like me, after my own heart. Hell, I guess I should of told you before, hell, but that movie wasn't ever about me, it was about you. I just played a supporting role. Hell, sorry about that book you thought we found. It was *their* idea, the crew's. Hell, they thought it would be great to see your face. Hey. I talked to the woman. She and the girl are both fine. You're lucky as hell. They'll help you recover. Don't worry about a thing. I already seed to it you got more credit up at the liquor store. You know me. Hell, I'm looking forward to seeing myself in the movie. Tell the crew I said hello. Remember, you and the woman and the girl come on over to the boat anytime.

Yours Very Truthfully,
Enoch Hunnicut

Frank Stanford was born August 1, 1948 somewhere in Mississippi. He was adopted by Dorothy Gilbert, a single woman, then Firestone's only female manager, shortly after his birth, and a few years later by her husband A.F. Stanford, a levee contractor. He grew up in Memphis, Tennessee and Mountain Home, Arkansas where his father retired. His most significant years of conventional education were spent at Subiaco, a Benedictine monastery and academy in the Ouachita Mountains of Arkansas. He attended the University of Arkansas and made his living as a land surveyor. He was twice married, lastly to the painter Ginny Crouch. He wrote many books, among them: *Constant Stranger, Field Talk, Shade, Ladies From Hell, Arkansas Benchstone, Crib Death, You, The Singing Knives* and *The Battlefield Where The Moon Says I Love You* a 542 page poem of extraordinary vision and power. His legacy of more than fifty complete manuscripts includes fiction, film scripts, interviews, essays and poems. He was the founding editor of Lost Roads Publishers. With his publisher Irv Broughton, he made documentary films, and together they produced a film about his own life and work titled *It Wasn't a Dream It Was A Flood* which won at the Third Annual Northwest Film & Video Festival in 1974. Frank Stanford died June 3, 1978 of self-inflicted gunshot wounds. The enormity of this loss is made bearable to those who loved the man and his work only by the enormity of his contribution as a poet. Finally there is the work.